Library of Congress Cataloging-in-Publication Data

Names: M. J. Nightengale
Title: Orion's Legacy
Identifiers: LCCN 2024900121
ISBN 979-8-9892106-2-6 (Paperback)

Published By: NP Arts, LLC.

Printed in the United States of America.

10 9 8 7 6 5 4 3 2 1

Orion's Tales

The Emerald Flame

Chapter 1

The sun was setting over the small village nestled at the foot of the Andes Mountains, casting long shadows that stretched across the dusty streets. In the midst of this twilight, a figure moved with silent grace, almost blending into the surroundings. Orion Nightshade, his dark cloak fluttering gently in the evening breeze, made his way through the village, his sharp eyes scanning the environment.

Orion's arrival in the village had not gone unnoticed. The local villagers, hardened by the harsh mountain life, watched the stranger with a mixture of curiosity and suspicion. Orion, however, was used to such receptions. His life as a thief and adventurer had taught him to be observant and cautious.

He stopped by a small tavern, its dimly lit interior promising both information and respite. As Orion pushed open the wooden door, a cacophony of voices and the smell of ale and roasting meat greeted him. He found a secluded corner and settled down, his eyes still surveying the room.

A server approached, her wary gaze flicking over Orion's unusual attire. "What can I get you, señor?" she asked.

"Just information," Orion replied, his voice low. "I'm looking for the Monastery of the Green Fire. What can you tell me about it?"

The server hesitated, then leaned in closer. "That monastery is a place of legends," she whispered. "They say it's guarded by monks who can bend nature to their will. But it's not a place for outsiders. Many have gone looking for it, few return."

Orion's interest piqued. This was exactly the kind of challenge he relished. "And what of the Serpent's Fang?" he prodded gently.

The server glanced around nervously. "They're a dangerous bunch, rumored to be searching for something powerful up there. Best to steer clear of them."

Thanking her, Orion pondered her words. The Serpent's Fang—a secret society he had encountered in hushed tales and whispers in dark alleys. Their sudden interest in the Monastery of the Green Fire was no coincidence.

Leaving the tavern, Orion decided to utilize his unique skills to gather more information. As night fell, he melded into the shadows, moving unseen through the village. He overheard conversations about strange occurrences in the mountains, and the increasing sightings of the Serpent's Fang members.

As he moved through the village, he felt a strange pull towards the mountains, as if an unseen force was guiding him. He knew that the key to unlocking his magical heritage lay within the monastery's ancient walls.

Orion's contemplative thoughts were interrupted when he stumbled upon a heated exchange in a dark alley. Two men, cloaked and menacing, were cornering a young woman.

"We know you've been snooping around, asking about the monastery," one of the men hissed.

Orion recognized the insignia on their cloaks—the Serpent's Fang. Without a second thought, he stepped from the shadows, his presence startling the men.

"Leave her alone," Orion commanded, his voice carrying an authoritative edge.

The men sneered, drawing their blades, but Orion was faster. With fluid movements honed by years of combat, he disarmed them, his shadow magic cloaking his actions in a blur of darkness.

As the men fled, the woman looked at Orion with wide, grateful eyes. "Thank you," she said. "I'm Elena. I've been trying to learn more about the Serpent's Fang. They've been lurking around here too often."

Orion regarded her thoughtfully. "Seems we have a common interest. I'm heading to the monastery. Perhaps we could help each other."

Elena nodded, a determined glint in her eyes. "I know the mountains well. I can guide you part of the way."

As they talked, Orion felt the pieces of the puzzle beginning to align. The journey ahead would be perilous, but he was ready. The secrets of the Emerald Flame and his own past were waiting to be unraveled.

With a new ally and a clear goal, Orion looked towards the towering Andes. The monastery beckoned, shrouded in mystery and danger. But within its ancient stone walls lay the answers he had been searching for his entire life.

And so, under the cover of night, with the whispers of destiny echoing in his ears, Orion Nightshade set forth on a journey that would test his skills, challenge his beliefs, and change the course of his life forever.

Chapter 2

The first light of dawn found Orion Nightshade and his newfound companion, Elena, at the edge of the village, facing the towering Andes. The mountains stood like ancient guardians, their peaks hidden in the clouds. Orion took a deep breath, feeling the cold mountain air fill his lungs. Beside him, Elena adjusted her pack, her eyes fixed on the path ahead.

"The monastery is said to be hidden deep within the mountains," she said, breaking the silence. "Few have attempted this journey and returned to tell the tale."

Orion nodded, hearing this already, as his eyes scanned the rugged terrain. "Then let's be among those few," he replied, his voice laced with determination.

They began their ascent, the path winding steeply upwards. The mountain's beauty was deceptive, its slopes treacherous. Every step was a test of endurance and will. Orion moved with agile ease, his years of thievery and adventure had prepared him for this. Elena, though not as experienced, proved to be a quick and able climber.

As they climbed, the landscape changed. The dense foliage gave way to rocky outcrops and steep cliffs. Orion's keen eyes spotted signs of wildlife – and something else. A subtle, almost imperceptible trace that someone had passed this way recently.

"We're not alone," he whispered to Elena, pointing at the faint tracks.

"Do you think it's the Serpent's Fang?" she asked, her hand instinctively reaching for the knife at her belt.

"Could be," Orion replied, his senses heightened. "Stay alert."

They pressed on, the mountain challenging them at every turn. The sun reached its zenith, and the air grew thinner. Orion felt the weight of his cloak and the pull of the amulet around his neck. He thought of the Emerald Flame, the power it held, and the secrets it might unlock about his past. His thoughts were a whirlwind of anticipation and apprehension.

As the afternoon waned, they encountered their first obstacle – a river, its waters fast and cold, cutting across their path. The bridge that once spanned it lay broken, its remnants swallowed by the churning water.

"We'll have to find another way across," Orion said, surveying the area.

"There," Elena pointed to a narrower part of the river upstream. "We can cross there."

The crossing was perilous. The rocks were slippery, and the water icy. Orion went first, his balance impeccable as he leaped from stone to stone. He reached the other side and extended a hand to Elena. She jumped, and for a fleeting moment, she faltered, but Orion's grip was firm, pulling her to safety.

"Thanks," she breathed, her heart racing.

They continued their journey, the shadows growing longer as the day aged. As evening approached, the first glimpse of their destination came into view – the silhouette of a structure, ancient and imposing, partially hidden by the mist.

"The Monastery of the Green Fire," Elena whispered in awe.

Orion's eyes narrowed as he observed it. "We'll approach under the cover of darkness. It'll give us an advantage."

Night fell, and with it, Orion's power grew. He felt at one with the shadows, his movements becoming even more fluid and silent. They reached the outskirts of the monastery, the structure looming large against the starlit sky. It was a fortress, built of stone, blending seamlessly with the mountain itself.

Orion and Elena crouched behind a large boulder, observing. There were no lights, no signs of life. The monastery appeared abandoned, yet something about it felt alive, as if the very stones were watching them.

"We should split up," Orion suggested. "Cover more ground. Look for a way in, but be careful. We don't know what we're dealing with here."

Elena nodded, and they parted ways, each melting into the darkness. Orion moved with purpose, every sense alert. He found a small entrance, partially hidden by overgrown vines. He slipped inside, his eyes adjusting to the darkness.

The interior was vast, the air heavy with the scent of incense and old stone. Orion treaded softly, his hand resting on the hilt of his dagger. The silence was oppressive, the only sound his own breathing and the distant drip of water.

Suddenly, he heard a faint sound – a whisper, almost inaudible. He froze, listening. The whisper grew louder, turning into a chant. It was coming from deep within the monastery.

Orion followed the sound, his heart pounding in his chest. The chant led him to a large chamber, its walls adorned with ancient symbols and flickering torches. And there, in the center of the chamber, a group of monks, their robes the color of the forest, were gathered in a circle.

Unseen, Orion watched as they chanted, their voices rising and falling in a hypnotic rhythm. He felt a strange energy in the room, a power that resonated with the amulet around his neck.

He had found the monks of the Green Fire. And with them, he knew, lay the answers he sought – and perhaps the key to unlocking the full potential of his powers.

Orion stepped back into the shadows, his mind racing. He needed to find Elena and plan their next move. The journey had just begun, and already, the mysteries of the Green Fire were unfolding before him.

Chapter 3

The monastery's ancient stone walls stood silent in the moonlight, casting long, foreboding shadows. Orion Nightshade, cloaked in darkness, felt a chill that wasn't just from the cold Andean air. Beside him, Elena whispered, "This place... it feels alive."

"You're not wrong," Orion replied softly, his eyes scanning the perimeter. "These walls have seen centuries pass. They hold secrets."

Their cautious approach was halted by the sudden appearance of hooded figures emerging from the shadows. The monks of the Green Fire, their movements graceful and silent, encircled Orion and Elena. One stepped forward, his age-lined face partially hidden beneath the hood.

"State your purpose," he said, his voice echoing slightly in the still night.

Orion met the monk's gaze. "I seek knowledge about the Emerald Flame," he declared.

The monks exchanged glances. "Many seek the Flame, few are worthy," the elder monk replied. "What makes you different?"

Orion reached into his cloak and revealed the ancient amulet. "This has been in my family for generations. It's linked to the Flame, and my heritage."

The monks murmured among themselves. The elder monk gestured for Orion and Elena to follow. "You will be tested," he said. "The Flame does not reveal itself to the unworthy."

They were led through a series of corridors, the monastery a labyrinth of stone and shadow. Finally, they entered a vast chamber, its walls adorned with intricate carvings depicting the natural world.

"Your first test," the elder monk began, "is one of combat. Our order values harmony with nature, but also the strength to protect it."

Two monks stepped forward, their stances poised and ready. Orion handed his cloak to Elena, feeling the weight of expectation. He faced his opponents, noting their balanced postures and calm demeanor.

The fight commenced with a sudden burst of speed. Orion's opponents were skilled, their attacks a blend of fluid motion and precision. But Orion was no stranger to combat. He moved with the shadows, his agility turning their strikes into near misses. The battle was a dance, each participant moving with lethal grace.

As the fight progressed, Orion found himself pushed to his limits. He realized this was more than a physical test – it was a challenge of spirit and mind. With a final, swift move, he disarmed his opponents, ending the confrontation.

The monks nodded in approval. "You have passed the first test," the elder monk acknowledged. "But physical prowess is not enough. The second test is one of the mind."

Orion and Elena were led to another chamber, this one filled with ancient texts and artifacts. "The history of our order is written here," the elder monk explained. "You must find the connection between your amulet and the Emerald Flame within these texts."

Orion stepped forward, his eyes scanning the ancient writings. Hours passed as he dove into the lore of the Green Fire, Elena assisting him. Finally, his eyes caught a passage describing a ritual involving a similar amulet, used to harness the Flame's power.

"I've found it," Orion exclaimed. The elder monk peered over his shoulder, reading the passage.

"You have shown wisdom and diligence," he said. "You are ready for the final test."

They were taken to the heart of the monastery, where a garden thrived, alive with nocturnal blooms and a serene pond. "Nature is the core of our existence," the elder monk spoke. "You must connect with it, understand its language."

Orion closed his eyes, feeling the life around him. He reached out with his senses, guided by the teachings in the texts. Gradually, he felt a connection, a harmony with the natural world. The garden seemed to respond, the pond's waters rippling gently, the flowers turning slightly towards him.

He opened his eyes, finding the monks watching him with a new respect. "You have passed our tests," the elder monk said. "You have shown strength, intelligence, and harmony with nature. You are worthy to learn about the Emerald Flame."

Orion felt a surge of triumph, but it was tempered by the weight of responsibility. The Flame was not just an artifact; it was a symbol of power and knowledge.

"As the day breaks, we will reveal to you the secrets of the Emerald Flame," the elder monk promised. "Prepare yourself, Orion Nightshade. Your journey has only just begun."

Orion and Elena were shown to a chamber to rest. As they settled, Orion pondered the tests and the challenges ahead. He knew that the Emerald Flame would bring him face-to-face with truths he might not be ready to confront. But he also knew that his journey was necessary, not just for himself, but for the mysteries that the Flame held within its ancient, fiery heart.

Chapter 4

The morning sun filtered through the high windows of the monastery, casting a golden hue on the ancient stones. Orion Nightshade, his eyes still adjusting to the light, followed Master Liang through the winding corridors. The air was thick with the scent of incense and age-old secrets.

Master Liang led Orion to a secluded chamber, its walls lined with intricate carvings and faded tapestries. At the center stood an altar, upon which lay a single, unlit candle.

"Orion Nightshade, you have proven yourself worthy to learn about the Emerald Flame," Master Liang began, his voice echoing softly. "But know this, the knowledge you seek is as perilous as it is powerful."

Orion nodded, his expression serious. "I am prepared," he said, his voice steady.

Master Liang lit the candle, and as the flame flickered to life, he began to speak. "The Emerald Flame is not just a source of magical energy; it is a sentient force, ancient and wise. It was discovered centuries ago by the first monks of the Green Fire. They learned to harness its power, but with great caution, for the Flame has a will of its own."

Orion listened intently, the light from the candle casting shadows across his face. "And the amulet I possess?" he asked.

"The amulet is a key," Master Liang replied, his eyes locking with Orion's. "It was crafted by the ancient monks to commune with the Flame. With it, you can harness the Flame's energy, but you must be in harmony with its spirit."

The conversation was interrupted by the arrival of Elena, escorted by Brother Tao. "Master Liang," she said, a hint of urgency in her voice. "We have discovered something troubling outside the monastery."

Master Liang turned, his expression growing grave. "What is it?"

Elena produced a small, intricately carved box. "We found this near the monastery's entrance. It bears the mark of the Serpent's Fang."

Master Liang took the box, examining it closely. "This is a grave sign," he said solemnly. "The Serpent's Fang is closer than we thought. They seek the Emerald Flame for their dark purposes."

Orion's jaw tightened. "Then we must act quickly. I must learn to control the Flame before they can reach it."

Master Liang nodded. "Indeed. But be warned, Orion. The path to mastering the Emerald Flame is fraught with danger. It will test you in ways you cannot imagine."

Orion met the monk's gaze. "I am ready for whatever comes."

Over the next few days, Orion underwent rigorous training. He meditated for hours, learning to attune his mind to the natural world. He practiced ancient rituals, each step bringing him closer to understanding the Emerald Flame.

But as Orion dove deeper into his training, he began to experience strange visions. Images of a past he did not recognize, voices whispering in a language he could not understand. The visions grew more intense, leaving him restless and troubled.

One night, as Orion sat alone in the chamber, the candle's flame dancing before him, he was overcome by a powerful vision. He saw a figure, cloaked in shadows, standing before the Emerald Flame. The figure turned, and Orion gasped. It was him, but older, wiser, his eyes burning with an inner light.

The vision spoke, its voice echoing in Orion's mind. "You are the key, Orion. The bridge between past and future. Embrace your destiny."

Orion awoke from the vision, his heart racing. He knew then that his connection to the Emerald Flame was more profound than he had realized. It was not just a source of power; it was a part of him, woven into the fabric of his being.

The following morning, Orion approached Master Liang. "I had a vision," he said, his voice steady despite the turmoil within. "I saw myself with the Emerald Flame. It spoke to me."

Master Liang regarded him with a knowing look. "The Flame has begun to reveal its secrets to you. You are nearing the end of your journey, Orion. Soon, you will face the ultimate test."

Orion nodded, a sense of determination rising within him. He was ready to face whatever the Flame had in store for him. He would master its power, not just for himself, but to protect it from those who would misuse it.

As Orion resumed his training, the monastery braced itself for the coming storm. The Serpent's Fang was drawing near, and time was running out. But Orion was no longer just a thief or an adventurer. He was a guardian of an ancient power, standing at the heart of the mountain, ready to face his destiny.

Chapter 5

Orion Nightshade stood alone in the Monastery of the Green Fire's ancient library, the weight of centuries around him. The air was dense with the scent of old parchment and wood. Shelves laden with texts and artifacts reached towards the high ceiling, casting long, intricate shadows in the candlelight.

He was searching for answers about his family's connection to the Emerald Flame. His fingers traced the spines of leather-bound books, each a repository of forgotten knowledge. Master Liang had granted him access to the library, understanding Orion's need to unravel the threads of his past.

As he doved deeper, a particular tome caught his eye. Its cover was adorned with the same intricate pattern as his amulet. With a sense of growing anticipation, Orion opened the book. The pages were filled with tales of ancient rituals and powerful families sworn to protect mystical artifacts. And there, amidst the legends, he found a reference to a family with an emblem identical to his amulet - the Nightshades.

Orion's heart quickened as he read about the Nightshades' role as guardians of the Emerald Flame, a legacy passed down through generations. But the tale took a dark turn – it spoke of a betrayal, a Nightshade who sought to use the Flame for personal gain, causing a rift that led to the family's downfall.

As he absorbed the story, a vision flashed before his eyes – a figure shrouded in darkness, standing before the Emerald Flame, his face a mirror of Orion's own. The vision was intense, almost overwhelming, but Orion forced himself to focus, to understand its meaning.

He was interrupted by Elena's entrance. "Orion, I've been looking for you," she said, her expression one of concern. "You've been in here for hours. Are you alright?"

Orion closed the book, the vision still vivid in his mind. "I found something," he said, his voice low. "About my family. We were guardians of the Flame, but something went wrong. There was a betrayal."

Elena stepped closer, her eyes filled with empathy. "That must be hard to come to terms with. But it doesn't define you, Orion. You're here to set things right."

Orion nodded, grateful for her words. "There's more to the story. I saw a vision, a shadow that looked like me, standing before the Flame."

Master Liang, who had been observing from the doorway, stepped into the room. "Visions are the Flame's way of communicating," he explained. "It's showing you your past, but also your potential future. The path of the guardian is fraught with challenges, but also great power."

Orion turned to Master Liang, determination in his eyes. "Then I will face whatever comes. I must learn more about the Flame and my family's connection to it."

Master Liang nodded approvingly. "Very well. But be cautious, Orion. The Flame's power is not to be taken lightly. And remember, the Serpent's Fang is still a threat."

The conversation was interrupted by Brother Tao rushing into the room. "Masters, something's happening at the monastery's edge. We need to see this."

They hurried outside, following Tao to the monastery's perimeter. The sight that greeted them was alarming – a group of hooded figures stood at the edge of the forest, their presence ominous in the fading light.

"The Serpent's Fang," Master Liang murmured, his expression turning grave.

Orion's hand went to the hilt of his dagger, his senses alert. "They're bold to come this close."

Elena's voice was steady, despite the tension. "What's our plan?"

"We need to fortify the monastery," Master Liang said. "Prepare for a possible attack. Orion, you and Elena should continue your research. The key to stopping them might lie in understanding the Flame."

As they headed back, Orion's mind was a whirl of thoughts. The legacy of his family, the power of the Emerald Flame, and the looming threat of the Serpent's Fang. Each piece of the puzzle was crucial, and he knew time was running out.

Back in the library, Orion and Elena pored over the texts, searching for anything that could help them understand the Flame's power and how to protect it. As night fell, Orion felt the weight of his heritage more than ever.

But amidst the uncertainty, one thing was clear – Orion Nightshade was no longer just seeking his past. He was fighting for a future where the Emerald Flame would be safe from those who sought to misuse its power. And in that fight, he was not alone. Elena and the monks of the Green Fire stood with him, each committed to protecting the legacy of the Emerald Flame.

Chapter 6

The night at the Monastery of the Green Fire was pierced by a sudden, chilling cry. Orion Nightshade, who had been deep in study, sprang to his feet, his instincts honed from a life of danger kicking in. Elena, equally alert, joined him as they rushed towards the source of the disturbance.

Outside, the serene moonlit night had erupted into chaos. Dark figures moved stealthily through the shadows, their cloaks bearing the unmistakable mark of the Serpent's Fang. The monastery, a bastion of peace and ancient wisdom, was under siege.

"Stay close," Orion whispered to Elena, drawing his dagger. His other hand instinctively reached for the amulet around his neck, drawing strength from its ancient power.

They saw Master Liang and Brother Tao engaged in battle with the intruders. The monks, usually so calm and collected, were fierce in their defense of the monastery. But it was clear they were outnumbered.

Orion leaped into action, his movements a blur as he moved from shadow to shadow. He struck swiftly, disarming one attacker after another with a grace that belied the lethalness of his strikes. Elena, not one to stand idly by, fought with a courage that matched any seasoned warrior, her own dagger finding its mark.

As they fought, Orion's mind raced. The Serpent's Fang's attack was no random act of aggression; they were here for the Emerald Flame. He needed to reach it before they did.

"Orion, we must protect the Flame!" yelled Master Liang, parrying a blow from an assailant.

Orion nodded, making a decision. "Elena, go with Master Liang. I'll hold them off."

Elena hesitated, her eyes betraying her concern. "Be careful, Orion."

With a nod, she and Master Liang made their way towards the inner sanctum, fighting off any attackers that came their way.

Orion turned his attention back to the battle, every sense heightened. He fought not just with his body but with his mind, predicting his enemies' moves, countering them with the precision of a master thief turned warrior.

The monastery's grounds were a maze of courtyards and gardens, and Orion used this to his advantage. He led a group of attackers on a chase, drawing them away from the inner sanctum. His plan was working, but it was also clear that the Serpent's Fang was not relenting.

In the midst of the chaos, a figure emerged from the shadows, their presence commanding. Zara Cortez, leader of the Serpent's Fang. Her eyes locked with Orion's, a cold smile playing on her lips.

"So, the prodigal son returns," she said, her voice laced with venom. "You cannot stop what is inevitable, Orion. The Flame will be ours."

Orion faced her, his stance unwavering. "Over my dead body," he replied, his voice steady.

The clash between Orion and Zara was a battle of not just brawn but wits. Each was a skilled fighter, but it was their knowledge of the other's past that added depth to their duel. Zara was relentless, her attacks a series of well-calculated moves designed to wear Orion down. But Orion was just as determined, his every strike fueled by the need to protect his heritage.

The fight took them across the monastery's grounds, a deadly dance under the moonlight. And just when it seemed Zara might gain the upper hand, Orion tapped into the power of his amulet. Shadows swirled around him, enhancing his movements, making him a ghostly figure of vengeance.

With a final, decisive move, Orion disarmed Zara, sending her sprawling to the ground. He stood over her, his dagger at her throat.

"This ends now," he said, his voice cold.

But before he could deliver the final blow, a loud explosion rocked the monastery. The inner sanctum. The Emerald Flame.

Orion's heart sank. He glanced at Zara, who was smirking despite her defeat. "You're too late," she hissed.

Orion raced towards the sanctum, fear and urgency driving him. As he arrived, he saw the unthinkable – the inner sanctum was in ruins, and the Emerald Flame was gone.

Master Liang and Elena were there, amidst the rubble, their faces etched with despair. "They took it," Master Liang said, his voice a mix of anger and sorrow.

Orion looked around at the destruction, the weight of failure heavy on his shoulders. The Flame was gone, and with it, a part of his heritage. But he knew this was not the end. It was only the beginning of a new, more perilous journey.

As dawn broke, the monastery was a scene of devastation. But amidst the ruin, there was a resolve. Orion, Elena, Master Liang, and the monks of the

Green Fire knew what they had to do. They would reclaim the Emerald Flame, no matter the cost.

The battle had ended, but the war for the Emerald Flame had just begun. And Orion Nightshade, once a lone thief in the shadows, was now a warrior at the heart of a much larger fight.

Chapter 7

In the aftermath of the attack, the Monastery of the Green Fire was a scene of somber reflection. The monks, led by Master Liang, worked tirelessly to repair the damage inflicted by the Serpent's Fang. Orion Nightshade, his mind heavy with the weight of the stolen Emerald Flame, joined their efforts, but his thoughts were elsewhere.

As night fell, Orion, Elena, Master Liang, and Brother Tao gathered in a secluded chamber, the air thick with the scent of burning incense and unspoken tension.

"We must understand their motives," Master Liang said gravely. "The Serpent's Fang wouldn't have attacked so brazenly without a clear objective. The Emerald Flame is powerful, but its true potential is unlocked only by one of our lineage."

Orion's eyes narrowed. "They must have someone capable of wielding it, or they believe they can coerce someone who can," he speculated.

Elena, her face shadowed by the flickering candlelight, added, "Their reach is far and wide. We need to uncover their plans if we are to have any hope of retrieving the Flame."

Brother Tao spoke up, "There have been whispers of a hidden stronghold where the Serpent's Fang gathers. A place shrouded in secrecy."

Orion looked at Master Liang. "I need to infiltrate their ranks, uncover their stronghold, and retrieve the Flame."

Master Liang's expression was stern, yet there was a hint of approval in his eyes. "It is a dangerous path, Orion. But it may be our only chance."

The plan was set. Orion would disguise himself and dive into the shadowy world of the Serpent's Fang. Elena insisted on accompanying him, arguing that her knowledge of the outside world would be invaluable. Reluctantly, Orion agreed.

The following night, under the guise of darkness, Orion and Elena set out. Dressed in cloaks that masked their identities, they journeyed into the heart of a nearby town rumored to have connections with the Serpent's Fang.

Their first stop was a dimly lit tavern, known to be a meeting place for unsavory characters. Orion's heightened senses were on alert, his hand never far from the hilt of his dagger.

They overheard hushed conversations, the name 'Serpent's Fang' uttered in fearful whispers. It didn't take long for Orion to recognize a pattern – a particular symbol, a snake encircling a flame, was being used as a sign of allegiance.

Using his charm and Elena's cunning, they gleaned information from the tavern's patrons. A name was mentioned, a place – the 'Cavern of Whispers' – where the Serpent's Fang was rumored to convene.

Their journey led them deeper into the underbelly of the town, each step taking them closer to danger. The Cavern of Whispers was located in a remote, desolate area, its entrance guarded by cloaked figures.

Orion and Elena approached cautiously, their disguises holding up under scrutiny. They were allowed entry, the heavy stone door groaning shut behind them.

Inside, the cavern was expansive, lit by torches casting eerie shadows on the walls. Figures in dark cloaks moved about, their conversations a low murmur. At the far end, a raised dais held a commanding presence – Zara Cortez.

She was speaking to her followers, her voice laced with authority. "The Emerald Flame is now in our possession. Soon, we will unlock its power and reshape the world in our image."

A chill ran down Orion's spine. The stakes were higher than he'd imagined.

Orion and Elena mingled among the crowd, careful to maintain their cover. They needed more information – the location of the Flame, the extent of the Serpent's Fang's plans.

As they gathered intelligence, a sudden commotion erupted at the cavern's entrance. The monastery's monks, led by Master Liang and Brother Tao, had launched a surprise attack.

Chaos ensued as battle lines were drawn. Orion and Elena were swept up in the fray, fighting back-to-back against the onslaught of Serpent's Fang members.

In the midst of the battle, Orion's gaze met Zara's. She smirked, a taunting gesture that fueled his resolve. He fought his way towards her, determined to confront her and reclaim the Flame.

But as he reached the dais, Zara was nowhere to be found. She had vanished, along with any trace of the Emerald Flame.

The monks, though outnumbered, fought valiantly, their discipline and training evident. Slowly, they turned the tide, the Serpent's Fang retreating into the shadows from which they had emerged.

As the dust settled, Orion, Elena, Master Liang, and Brother Tao regrouped. The Cavern of Whispers was now empty, a hollow echo of the secrets it once held.

"We were too late," Orion said, frustration evident in his voice. "Zara has the Flame, and we're no closer to stopping her."

Master Liang placed a reassuring hand on his shoulder. "We may not have retrieved the Flame, but we have shown the Serpent's Fang that they cannot act with impunity. We will find them, Orion. And we will stop them."

As they left the cavern, Orion looked up at the stars, a sense of determination rising within him. The battle for the Emerald Flame was far from over, and he would not rest until it was safe once again.

The journey ahead was uncertain, fraught with danger and deception. But Orion Nightshade, once a solitary figure in the shadows, was now part of something greater – a fight for the very balance of power in the world. The path ahead was unclear, but his resolve was unwavering. The Serpent's Fang would be stopped, no matter the cost.

Chapter 8

Orion Nightshade, cloaked in the guise of a Serpent's Fang member, stood beside Elena in the shadowy outskirts of a clandestine meeting. Their infiltration into the enemy's ranks was a daring gamble, one that placed them in the lion's den of the very force they sought to thwart.

As they mingled with the throng of hooded figures, Orion's senses were on high alert, his eyes scanning the dimly lit hall for any sign of the Emerald Flame or clues to its whereabouts. Elena, equally vigilant, whispered, "Remember, we're here to gather information, not to engage."

Their conversation was interrupted by the arrival of Zara Cortez, her commanding presence silencing the room. "Tonight, we consolidate our power," she proclaimed, her voice resonant with authority. "The Emerald Flame will soon be ours to control, and with it, the world will bend to our will."

Orion's grip on his concealed dagger tightened. The stakes were higher than ever.

As the meeting progressed, Orion and Elena gathered crucial information about the Serpent's Fang's network and their impending plans. It became evident that the ceremony to unlock the Emerald Flame's power was imminent and would take place at a location known only to the inner circle.

Orion knew they needed to penetrate deeper into the Serpent's Fang's hierarchy. He made a calculated decision to approach one of the members, feigning allegiance to their cause. His ploy was a success, leading him to a private discussion with one of the lieutenants.

During the conversation, Orion skillfully steered the topic towards the ceremony. The lieutenant, believing Orion to be a loyal member, divulged the location – an ancient fortress hidden in the Andean highlands.

With the critical information in hand, Orion and Elena discreetly exited the meeting, their minds racing with the urgency of their mission. They needed to relay this information to Master Liang and prepare a plan to intercept the ceremony.

Their journey back to the Monastery of the Green Fire was fraught with peril, as they navigated through the treacherous terrain and evaded patrols of the Serpent's Fang.

Upon their return, they convened with Master Liang and Brother Tao. Orion laid out their findings, his voice steady despite the exhaustion that clung to him. "The ceremony is to take place at an ancient fortress in the Andes. We must act quickly if we are to prevent them from unlocking the Flame's full potential."

Master Liang nodded gravely. "We will need to mobilize our forces and strike with precision. The fate of the Emerald Flame and the balance of power it holds is in our hands."

Elena added, "We'll need to be strategic. The Serpent's Fang will be heavily guarded, and they won't hesitate to use the Flame if they sense our approach."

The monastery sprang into action, preparing for the impending confrontation. Orion, though weary, felt a resolute determination. The journey had brought him face to face with the darkest elements of his past, but it had also ignited a fire within him – a desire to protect the legacy of the Emerald Flame and thwart the sinister ambitions of the Serpent's Fang.

As night fell, Orion stood at the edge of the monastery, gazing into the starlit sky. The path ahead was fraught with danger, but he was no longer the solitary figure who had first set out on this quest. He was part of something greater – a fight for the very soul of the world.

Elena joined him, her presence a reassuring comfort. "We'll face this together," she said, her voice resolute.

Orion nodded, his eyes reflecting the resolve that burned within him. "Together," he echoed.

The stage was set for a battle that would decide the fate of the Emerald Flame. Orion Nightshade, once a mere shadow in the night, was now a beacon of hope in the darkness, ready to confront the looming threat and protect a legacy that transcended time itself.

Chapter 9

The night was deep and full of secrets as Orion Nightshade sat in the cloistered chamber of the Monastery of the Green Fire, his thoughts a tumultuous sea. The information gleaned from their infiltration into the Serpent's Fang had set a new, urgent course of action. But among the whispers of strategy and planning, a nagging doubt gnawed at Orion's mind, a suspicion that there was a traitor among them.

Master Liang, Brother Tao, Elena, and Orion gathered around an ancient table, maps and scrolls spread before them. Their discussion was intense, focused on thwarting the Serpent's Fang's plans to utilize the Emerald Flame.

"It's not just the ceremony we need to worry about," Orion said, his eyes dark with concern. "There's something else. I fear there's a traitor in our midst."

The room fell silent, the weight of his words hanging heavy in the air. Master Liang's eyes narrowed. "What leads you to believe this?"

Orion recounted his observations during their last encounter with the Serpent's Fang, how certain information seemed to be anticipated by their enemies. "It's as if they knew our moves before we made them."

The suspicion cast a shadow over the group, each member suddenly aware of the delicate trust that bound them. Elena's gaze met Orion's, a flicker of unease in her eyes. "We need to find out who it is before it's too late."

The following day, under the guise of normalcy, Orion and Elena began their subtle investigation, watching the monastery's inhabitants with a discreet but discerning eye. Their inquiry led them to a series of clandestine observations and covert conversations.

It was during a late-night vigil that Orion caught the first real clue. A shadowy figure met with a known associate of the Serpent's Fang at the edge of the monastery grounds. The figure was hooded, but Orion recognized the gait, the posture. It was Brother Tao.

Heart pounding, Orion relayed the information to Master Liang and Elena. The revelation struck them with the force of a betrayal too deep to fathom.

"We must confront him," Master Liang said, his voice heavy with sorrow.

The confrontation was swift and tense. Brother Tao, cornered and unable to flee, finally confessed. His betrayal was born not of malice but of coercion. The Serpent's Fang had his family and had threatened their lives unless he complied.

The air was thick with a mix of anger, betrayal, and pity. Master Liang, though pained by the revelation, knew they had to act quickly. "We have no time for retribution. Our focus must remain on stopping the Serpent's Fang and recovering the Emerald Flame."

Plans were quickly revised, taking into account the compromised security. Orion, his resolve hardened by the sting of betrayal, knew that the path ahead would be fraught with even greater dangers.

As the night deepened, Orion and Elena prepared for their journey to the ancient fortress where the ceremony was to take place. Their farewell was brief, the urgency of their mission leaving no room for prolonged goodbyes.

The journey to the fortress was treacherous, the path fraught with peril. As they neared their destination, the silhouette of the fortress loomed against the starlit sky, a foreboding monument to the power and ambition of the Serpent's Fang.

Orion and Elena approached with caution, aware that the fortress would be heavily guarded. Using a combination of stealth and cunning, they infiltrated the fortress's outer defenses, making their way towards the inner sanctum where the ceremony was to take place.

Their progress was slow, hindered by the need for utmost stealth. Every shadow could conceal an enemy, every sound could betray their presence.

As they edged closer to the heart of the fortress, the sounds of the ceremony began to reach them, a low, ominous chant that spoke of ancient rituals and dark magic.

Orion's hand gripped the hilt of his dagger, the familiar weight a reminder of the battles he had fought and the ones that lay ahead. Elena, equally determined, moved silently at his side, her own weapons at the ready.

They were close now, the fate of the Emerald Flame hanging in the balance. Orion knew that the confrontation with the Serpent's Fang would be inevitable and that the coming hours would test him as never before.

But he was ready. Ready to face the darkness, to protect the legacy of the Emerald Flame, and to confront the shadows that had long been a part of his own soul. The night was deep, but Orion Nightshade was deeper still, a warrior born of shadow and light, poised to strike at the heart of his enemy's domain.

Chapter 10

Under the cover of darkness, Orion Nightshade and Elena approached the ancient fortress, the location of the Emerald Flame. The fortress, nestled among the high Andes peaks, was an imposing structure, its walls steeped in history and dark magic. They moved stealthily, aware of the grave danger that lay ahead.

As they infiltrated the fortress, they found themselves in a labyrinth of corridors and secret passages. The air was thick with anticipation, the energy of the Emerald Flame palpable even through the fortress's stone walls.

Their search led them to a grand chamber, where they hid in the shadows, observing the Serpent's Fang preparing for the ceremony. The room was adorned with ancient symbols and lit by flickering torches, casting eerie shadows on the walls.

In the center of the chamber, on a raised dais, sat the Emerald Flame. It pulsed with a powerful energy, its green light casting an otherworldly glow. Orion felt a connection to it, a pull that was both exhilarating and terrifying.

Zara Cortez stood before the Flame, her presence commanding and malevolent. She began chanting in an ancient tongue, her voice echoing through the chamber. The members of the Serpent's Fang gathered around, their eyes fixed on the Flame with fervent zeal.

Orion knew they had to act fast. He signaled to Elena, and they prepared to disrupt the ceremony. As they stepped out of the shadows, a sudden, intense energy surged through the room. The Emerald Flame flared brightly, and an invisible force threw them back.

Orion struggled to his feet, his head spinning. The Flame's power was unlike anything he had ever felt. It was a raw, primal force, and it was clear that Zara Cortez was moments away from unlocking its full potential.

In a desperate bid, Orion lunged forward, using his shadow magic to blend into the darkness. He moved with agility, weaving through the members of the Serpent's Fang, his eyes fixed on the Emerald Flame.

As he reached the dais, Zara Cortez turned to face him, her eyes filled with fury. "You are too late, Nightshade," she hissed. "The power of the Emerald Flame will be mine!"

A fierce battle ensued. Orion fought with every ounce of his strength and skill, his shadow magic pitted against Zara's dark sorcery. Elena joined the fray, her bravery and cunning a vital force in the struggle.

The chamber became a whirlwind of energy, spells clashing with the force of colliding storms. The members of the Serpent's Fang were thrown into chaos, their ceremony disrupted by the unexpected assault.

In the midst of the battle, Orion saw his chance. He leaped towards the Emerald Flame, his hand outstretched. As he touched it, a shockwave of energy coursed through his body, an overwhelming rush of power and knowledge.

Visions flashed before his eyes – memories of ancient guardians, secrets of his lineage, and the true potential of the Emerald Flame. He understood now; the Flame was not just a source of power – it was a beacon of balance, a guardian of the natural order.

With newfound strength, Orion faced Zara Cortez. Their final confrontation was epic, a clash of light and darkness. As they battled, Orion realized the key to defeating her lay in harnessing the Flame's energy, not as a weapon, but as a force of equilibrium.

With a powerful incantation, Orion channeled the Emerald Flame's energy, its light enveloping Zara Cortez. She screamed in defiance, but her dark magic was no match for the purifying power of the Flame. With a final, blinding flash, she was defeated, her plans to control the Flame thwarted.

Exhausted but triumphant, Orion and Elena stood amidst the aftermath. The Emerald Flame, now calm, glowed softly, its energy balanced once more.

Master Liang and the monks arrived, having followed Orion and Elena to the fortress. They gazed upon the Flame with reverence, understanding the significance of what had transpired.

Orion turned to the Flame, feeling a deep connection to his heritage and the legacy it represented. He had unlocked its secrets, but more importantly, he had protected its sanctity.

As dawn broke over the Andes, a new chapter in Orion's journey began. The battle was over, but his quest was far from finished. With the Emerald Flame secure and his powers fully realized, Orion Nightshade set his sights on the horizon, ready to face whatever mysteries and adventures lay ahead. His legacy, like the Flame, was a light in the darkness, guiding him on the path of a hero.

Chapter 11

In the aftermath of the tumultuous battle at the fortress, the air was thick with the scent of charred stone and the echoes of magical energies dissipating. Orion Nightshade stood in the center of the ruins, his eyes reflecting the subdued glow of the Emerald Flame.

The weight of his victory and the newfound power coursing through him was palpable. He felt an intense connection to the Flame, a symbiosis that was both empowering and daunting. Around him, the members of the Serpent's Fang lay defeated, their plans thwarted by Orion's bravery and cunning.

Elena approached him, her expression a mix of awe and concern. "Orion, are you alright?" she asked, her voice tinged with worry.

Orion turned to her, his eyes still ablaze with the power of the Flame. "I am more than alright, Elena. I feel... awakened," he replied, his voice resonating with an underlying strength.

Master Liang and Brother Tao joined them, their faces etched with relief and pride. "You have done well, Orion," Master Liang said, his voice calm and steady. "You have protected the Emerald Flame and, in doing so, have unlocked the full potential of your powers."

Orion nodded, understanding the responsibility that came with such power. "I know what I must do now. The path ahead is clear to me," he said, his gaze firm.

The group made their way back to the Monastery of the Green Fire, where they were greeted with reverence and gratitude by the other monks. News of Orion's victory had spread, and he was hailed as a hero, a protector of the ancient and mystical order.

In the quiet sanctity of the monastery, Orion took time to reflect on his journey. The revelations about his heritage, the depth of his powers, and the destiny that awaited him were overwhelming, yet he felt a sense of purpose like never before.

One evening, as the sun set over the Andes, casting a golden hue over the mountains, Master Liang approached Orion. "Your journey is far from over, young Nightshade," he said, his eyes gleaming with wisdom. "The Emerald Flame was just the beginning. There are other mystical artifacts, each with their own power and legacy."

Orion listened intently, the flames of adventure and discovery igniting within him. "I am ready, Master Liang. I will seek out these artifacts and protect them from those who wish to misuse their power," he declared, his voice resolute.

Master Liang nodded, a smile playing on his lips. "I have no doubt, Orion. But remember, with great power comes great responsibility. You must remain true to your path and use your abilities for the greater good."

Orion spent the next few days at the monastery, honing his skills and deepening his understanding of his powers. He trained with Brother Tao, who had become a close friend and ally, and spent hours in conversation with Elena, who had been instrumental in his quest.

As the day of his departure neared, Orion felt a mix of excitement and apprehension. He knew that the road ahead would be fraught with danger and challenges, but he was ready to face them head-on.

On the morning of his departure, the monks of the Green Fire gathered to bid him farewell. Master Liang placed a hand on Orion's shoulder, imparting a final piece of wisdom. "Remember, Orion, the balance of power is delicate. Use your gifts wisely and justly."

Orion nodded, his heart swelling with gratitude and determination. He turned to Elena and Brother Tao, a smile on his face. "Let's begin the next chapter of our adventure," he said, his eyes sparkling with anticipation.

With a final look at the monastery, Orion set off into the sunrise, his cloak billowing behind him. The Emerald Flame's legacy was now part of him, and he was ready to embrace his destiny, wherever it may lead. The world was vast, and the mysteries it held were waiting to be uncovered. Orion Nightshade, the thief turned hero, was ready to face them all.

Chapter 12

Orion Nightshade stood at the edge of the Monastery of the Green Fire, gazing out over the lush expanse of the Andean landscape, bathed in the golden light of dawn. The events of the past weeks felt like a whirlwind, a storm of revelations and confrontations that had reshaped his very existence.

Elena joined him, her presence a comforting constant in the chaos of his life. "It's beautiful, isn't it?" she remarked, her eyes reflecting the serene beauty of the sunrise.

"It is," Orion replied, his voice tinged with a mix of nostalgia and anticipation. "It's hard to believe that not long ago, I was unaware of the depths of my heritage and the power I possess."

Master Liang approached them, his steps silent and measured. "Orion, the path you have chosen is fraught with challenges, but it is also filled with immense potential. You have shown great courage and strength," he said, his wise eyes meeting Orion's.

Orion nodded in respect. "I have learned much from you, Master Liang, and from the Monastery. I am ready to embark on my journey, to uncover the truths about my family and the mystical artifacts."

Elena looked at him, concern etched on her face. "Are you sure about this, Orion? The world beyond these mountains is vast and unpredictable."

Orion turned to her, his dark eyes resolute. "I must do this, Elena. There are mysteries out there waiting to be solved, and I feel a responsibility to seek them out. But I won't be alone," he added, glancing at Brother Tao, who stood a few steps away, an eager smile on his face.

Brother Tao stepped forward. "I'm with you, Orion. Wherever this adventure leads, I'm ready to face it," he declared, his youthful enthusiasm infectious.

Orion smiled, grateful for the camaraderie and support. "Then let's not delay any further. Our journey awaits."

The group made their preparations, gathering essential supplies and bidding farewell to the monks and villagers who had become their friends and allies. The air was filled with a sense of excitement and uncertainty as they embarked on their new adventure.

As they trekked down the mountain path, Orion reflected on the lessons he had learned and the battles he had fought. The Emerald Flame had unlocked his powers, but it was his determination and courage that had truly defined him.

The journey took them through verdant forests and across rugged terrain, each step leading them further into the unknown. They encountered challenges and obstacles, but together, they overcame them with skill and teamwork.

As days turned into weeks, their bond strengthened, and they faced each new trial with a sense of purpose and resolve. Orion's leadership and magical abilities proved invaluable, guiding them through dangers and revealing hidden truths.

One evening, as they camped under the stars, Orion opened up to his companions. "I used to think of my powers as a curse, a shadow hanging over my life. But now, I see them as a gift, a chance to make a difference in this world."

Elena smiled at him, her eyes shining in the firelight. "You've come a long way, Orion. You're not the same man who walked into that village at the foot of the Andes. You've grown, and you've helped us grow too."

Orion gazed into the fire, the flames dancing and casting a warm glow on their faces. "There's so much more out there, so many secrets to uncover. I feel like we're just scratching the surface."

Brother Tao nodded, his eyes full of wonder. "The world is a mysterious place, but with you leading the way, I think we can unravel some of its mysteries."

As the fire crackled and the night deepened, Orion looked up at the stars, feeling a deep connection to the universe and its endless mysteries. He knew that their journey was far from over, that there were many paths yet to explore and many truths yet to uncover.

With the Emerald Flame's power within him and his loyal companions by his side, Orion Nightshade was ready to face whatever lay ahead. The legacy of the flame had ignited a new chapter in his life, one filled with adventure, discovery, and the unyielding quest for knowledge.

As the first light of dawn crept over the horizon, Orion stood up, a determined look in his eyes. "Let's continue our journey. Destiny awaits, and we have many paths to explore."

With that, Orion, Elena, and Brother Tao set off into the breaking day, their spirits high and their hearts full of hope. The future was unwritten, but they were ready to write their own stories, to leave their mark on the tapestry of time.

Orion's legacy, born from the shadows and forged in the flames, was just beginning.

The Sapphire Sea

Chapter 1

In the heart of the moonlit harbor, a ship swayed gently on the Pacific's subtle swell. Its dark sails, kissed by starlight, bore the emblem of a shadowy hawk. Standing at the helm, Orion Nightshade gazed into the horizon, where the sea merged with the night sky. The air was thick with salt and anticipation. His ship, the Nightwing, was ready to embark on a journey shrouded in mystery and danger – the search for the Sapphire Sea Monastery.

Orion's thoughts were a turbulent sea of their own. He remembered the tales his mother whispered in his childhood, stories of a hidden island where water flowed not just in rivers, but through the very air, held and shaped by those who understood its secrets. These stories, once a bedtime fantasy, now held the key to understanding his own magical heritage.

"Captain Nightshade, we are ready to set sail," announced a stern voice. It was Eris, his first mate, a woman of few words but unshakable loyalty. Her presence was a comfort, a fixed point in the ever-shifting tides of his life.

"Set the course, Eris. We sail for the unknown," Orion replied, his voice steady as the wind that began to fill their sails.

As the Nightwing cut through the water, Orion reflected on his past adventures. Each had been a step in his journey, a journey that had led him here, to the brink of the world's edge, chasing a dream that was as elusive as the morning mist. The Sapphire Sea Monastery was a place of legend, a haven for those who mastered the art of water magic. And within its ancient walls, Orion hoped to find answers to the mysteries of his shadow magic, which had begun to show unusual, almost aquatic, characteristics.

The night passed in silence, the ship slicing through the water like a shadow. Orion stood watch, his eyes never straying far from the dark horizon. The sea seemed to whisper to him, its voice a blend of warning and welcome.

Dawn broke with a palette of fiery oranges and soft pinks, painting the sky in a light that seemed to promise new beginnings. Orion, however, felt a knot of apprehension in his stomach. He knew that the journey ahead would not be a simple one. The Pacific was vast and unforgiving, and the hidden island would not reveal itself easily.

As the sun climbed higher, the crew busied themselves with their duties, their movements a well-rehearsed dance of efficiency and skill. Orion, meanwhile, retreated to his cabin. The walls were lined with maps and charts, the table cluttered with books on ancient magic and forgotten islands.

He unrolled a parchment, its edges worn and its surface marked with countless annotations. This was the map that had set him on his current course, a gift from an old sage who had seen in Orion a worthy seeker. The map was a puzzle, its clues written in riddles and cryptic symbols. Orion had spent countless nights trying to decipher its secrets.

A knock on the door pulled him from his thoughts. It was Eris, her expression unusually grave.

"Captain, there's something you should see," she said, her voice tense.

Orion followed her to the deck, where the crew had gathered, their eyes fixed on the horizon. There, emerging from the morning mist, was a sight that made Orion's heart skip a beat – the silhouette of an island, its peaks rising like jagged teeth against the sky.

"Is that...?" Eris began, but Orion was already moving, his eyes alight with a mixture of awe and determination.

"It has to be," he said. "Prepare for landing. Our quest begins here."

As the Nightwing approached the island, Orion felt a connection, a pull that resonated deep within his soul. This was no ordinary place; it was a piece of his history, a part of his destiny.

The island was covered in lush greenery, its beaches golden and inviting. But it was the air that caught Orion's attention – it seemed to shimmer, as if charged with unseen energy. He knew then that they had found it, the hidden sanctuary of the Sapphire Sea Monastery.

Stepping onto the shore, Orion felt a sense of completion, as if he had returned home after a long journey. But he also knew that this was just the beginning. The island held secrets, secrets that would challenge him, change him, and ultimately, reveal the true extent of his powers.

And so, with the whispers of the Sapphire Sea echoing in his ears, Orion Nightshade stepped forward into a destiny that had been waiting for him all his life. The journey ahead was uncertain, but one thing was clear – it would be a tale worth telling.

Chapter 2

The sun climbed higher, casting a warm glow over the hidden island as Orion Nightshade and his crew disembarked from the Nightwing. The island, an emerald jewel amidst the sapphire expanse of the sea, was both mesmerizing and foreboding. Its dense jungle whispered secrets, and the air hummed with a magic that Orion felt in his very bones.

Eris, ever the pragmatist, was the first to break the silence. "We should set up a base camp. The island is larger than it appears, and we don't know what we're up against."

Orion nodded, his eyes scanning the treeline. "Agreed. But we must be cautious. This place is not just an island; it's a guardian of mysteries."

As they ventured deeper, the island revealed its unique flora and fauna. Exotic birds with iridescent feathers flitted between giant ferns and towering trees. The air was heavy with the scent of unknown flowers, and the sound of distant, unseen creatures echoed through the underbrush.

It was while examining a particularly unusual flower, its petals shimmering with an inner light, that Orion first sensed it – a subtle shift in the shadows, as if they were being watched. He turned swiftly, his hand reaching for the amulet around his neck, but there was nothing there, only the flicker of sunlight through the leaves.

"Did you see that, Eris?" he asked, his voice low.

Eris, who had been surveying their surroundings, shook her head. "See what?"

"Never mind," Orion murmured, but his mind was alert, his senses heightened. The island was alive, and not just with the creatures that called it home.

They set up a temporary camp at the edge of a clearing, near a stream with crystal-clear water. As the crew busied themselves, Orion took a moment to reflect on the journey that had brought him here. He thought of his mother, her stories of water and magic, and wondered if she had ever walked these very paths.

As night fell, the island transformed. The moon cast a silvery light, turning the jungle into a realm of shadows and whispers. Orion sat by the campfire, his eyes lost in the dance of the flames. Eris joined him, her expression thoughtful.

"What do you think we'll find here, Orion?" she asked.

"I'm not sure," he admitted. "But I feel that the answers I seek are close. The monastery, my mother's past, the evolution of my magic – they're all intertwined with this island."

The night passed in a restless vigil. Orion's dreams were filled with visions of water and shadows, and a sense that something ancient and powerful was calling to him.

The next morning, as they ventured deeper into the island, the sense of mystery only deepened. They came across ruins overgrown with vines, the remnants of what must have been a grand structure. The stones were carved with symbols that resonated with Orion's amulet, causing it to glow faintly.

"What do you make of this, Orion?" Eris asked, examining the carvings.

"It's a language of magic, old and forgotten by most. These ruins are a sign. We're on the right path," Orion replied, his fingers tracing the symbols.

Their exploration took them through landscapes that seemed to defy reality. They encountered a lake that mirrored the sky so perfectly that it was impossible to tell where the water ended and the heavens began. In a dense grove, they found flowers that sang when touched, their melodies haunting and beautiful.

But it was in the heart of the island that they found the most astonishing sight. A waterfall, cascading from an impossible height, its waters shimmering with a thousand hues of blue and green. And behind the veil of water, a cave.

"This must be it," Orion breathed, his heart racing. "The entrance to the Sapphire Sea Monastery."

But as they approached, a sense of foreboding washed over him. The island had revealed its heart, but the secrets it guarded were not given freely. The shadows seemed to deepen, and a chill ran down Orion's spine.

He turned to Eris, his resolve clear in his eyes. "We must be prepared for anything. The mysteries of the Sapphire Sea are within our grasp, but they will not be easily unveiled."

Together, they stepped toward the waterfall, ready to uncover the secrets that lay beyond. The Island of Shadows had welcomed them, but it would not yield its mysteries without a test. Orion Nightshade, with the legacy of his lineage and the weight of his quest, was ready to face whatever lay ahead.

Chapter 3

The hidden cave behind the waterfall unveiled a passage that wound deep into the heart of the island. Orion Nightshade, with Eris and a select few of his crew, ventured into the darkness, their torches casting flickering shadows on the ancient walls. The air was cool and damp, filled with the scent of moss and earth.

As they dove deeper, the passage opened into a vast cavern, its walls glistening with moisture. Stalactites and stalagmites formed natural sculptures, creating an otherworldly landscape. At the center of the cavern, a pool of water reflected the torchlight, its surface still and mysterious.

"It's like stepping into another world," Eris whispered, her voice echoing softly.

Orion felt a strange connection to this place, a sense of déjà vu that he couldn't quite place. His amulet pulsed gently against his chest, as if resonating with the energy of the cavern.

They explored the cavern, finding inscriptions and carvings that spoke of water and magic. But it was a simple, unassuming doorway at the far end that drew Orion's attention. He approached it, feeling a magnetic pull.

As he touched the door, it swung open silently, revealing a chamber beyond. Inside, they found an old man sitting cross-legged on the floor, his eyes closed in meditation. He was clothed in simple robes, his hair and beard long and white.

Orion stepped forward, a sense of reverence washing over him. "Are you the guardian of this place?" he asked.

The old man opened his eyes, and they sparkled with wisdom. "I am Sage Aelius, keeper of the island's lore. And you, Orion Nightshade, are the one I have been waiting for."

Orion's heart skipped a beat. "How do you know my name?"

Aelius smiled. "The island speaks to those who listen. It has told me of your arrival, of your quest for understanding. You seek the Sapphire Sea Monastery and the secrets it holds."

"Yes," Orion confirmed. "I believe it's connected to my mother's past and to the nature of my magic."

Aelius nodded. "The monastery is a place of great power, a nexus where the water's essence and magic converge. Your mother, she was a part of this place, her spirit intertwined with the island."

Orion felt a surge of emotion. "My mother... was she from here?"

"In a manner of speaking," Aelius said. "She was like you, a seeker of truth, drawn to the island's mysteries. Her journey here shaped her, just as it will shape you."

Eris, who had been listening intently, spoke up. "But why is this place hidden? Why guard its secrets so closely?"

"The knowledge here is powerful and dangerous in the wrong hands," Aelius replied. "It must be protected, for it can alter the very essence of nature."

Orion pondered Aelius's words, feeling the weight of his heritage. "And the Sapphire Sea Monastery? How do we find it?"

"The path will reveal itself to those who are worthy," Aelius said cryptically. "But be warned, the way is perilous, and you are not the only one seeking its power."

Orion understood the implicit warning – Captain Maelstrom and her pirates were also on the island, their intentions far from noble.

"Thank you, Sage Aelius. We will be cautious," Orion said, a determined glint in his eyes.

As they left the chamber, Aelius called out, "Orion, remember, the island holds not just secrets, but also answers. Your journey here is more than a search for the monastery; it's a quest for self-discovery."

Back in the cavern, Orion felt a newfound resolve. The echoes of the past were calling to him, and he knew that his journey on the island was about to take a deeper, more personal turn.

Eris glanced at Orion, sensing the change in him. "What's our next move?"

Orion looked back at the pool in the center of the cavern, where the still water seemed to hold untold depths. "We explore the island, uncover its secrets. The path to the monastery will reveal itself in time. For now, we must learn all we can and be ready for whatever challenges lie ahead."

As they retraced their steps back to the surface, the mysteries of the island hung heavily around them. Orion knew that the journey ahead would test him in ways he couldn't yet imagine. But he was ready. The echoes of the past were guiding him, and he would follow them wherever they led, into the heart of the Sapphire Sea.

Chapter 4

Orion Nightshade and his crew had barely begun to explore the dense jungles of the island when the air suddenly filled with the unmistakable sound of rustling leaves and snapping twigs. They were not alone. The crew tensely gripped their weapons, eyes scanning the dense foliage.

"Prepare yourselves," Orion whispered, his hand instinctively moving to the amulet at his neck. The shadows around them seemed to deepen, responding to his silent command.

From the underbrush emerged a band of rugged individuals, their eyes fierce and their intentions clear. They were Captain Leandra Maelstrom's pirates, recognizable by their tattered sea-worn clothes and the malicious gleam in their eyes.

"Orion Nightshade, the shadow thief," a gruff voice called out. It was Captain Maelstrom herself, stepping forward with a confident stride. Her presence was commanding, her gaze sharp as she eyed Orion. "You're far from your shadowy alleys now."

Orion stood tall, his demeanor calm but alert. "Maelstrom. I should have known you'd be drawn to the Sapphire Sea's secrets."

"Aye, and I won't let you or your trinkets stand in my way," she retorted, her hand resting on the hilt of her sword.

The standoff was brief but intense. Then, with a subtle nod from Maelstrom, the pirates attacked. The clash was immediate and fierce, swords clashing against swords, the air filled with the sounds of battle.

Orion moved with a dancer's grace, his shadow magic flowing through him. He was a blur of movement, his attacks precise and lethal. But Maelstrom's crew was well-trained and ruthless, their numbers overwhelming.

As the fight ensued, Orion noticed something different about his powers. The shadows seemed to ripple and flow like water, their movements more fluid than ever before. He felt a deep connection to the island's energy, enhancing his abilities in ways he had never experienced.

Eris fought fiercely at his side, her skills honed from years on the sea. "Orion, we need to push them back!"

Nodding, Orion focused his energy, extending his arms outward. The shadows responded, expanding and swirling around the pirates, disorienting them and giving Orion and his crew the upper hand.

Maelstrom, observing the change in Orion's magic, realized they were outmatched. "Retreat!" she barked, and her crew began to withdraw, disappearing into the jungle as swiftly as they had appeared.

After the pirates had fled, the crew gathered around Orion. "Captain, your powers..." Eris began, her expression a mix of awe and concern.

Orion looked at his hands, the shadows still swirling around his fingers. "The island is changing me, strengthening my connection to the shadows. But now they flow like water."

"It's the influence of the Sapphire Sea," a crew member muttered. "I've heard tales of this place, how it can change a man."

Orion knew he was evolving, his magic taking on a new form. This island, with its deep connection to water and its mystical essence, was reshaping his abilities. It was both exhilarating and terrifying.

"We must continue our search for the monastery," Orion declared. "But be on your guard. Maelstrom won't give up easily."

As they ventured deeper into the island, the sense of mystery and danger grew. The lush greenery concealed unknown threats, and the air was thick with the promise of more encounters.

That night, as they camped under the stars, Orion couldn't help but ponder over his encounter with Maelstrom. She was a formidable foe, her past shrouded in as much mystery as his. Their paths were intertwined, bound by a rivalry that went deeper than mere competition for the monastery's secrets.

Eris approached him, her face illuminated by the campfire. "Orion, we need to be careful. Maelstrom is cunning and ruthless. She won't stop until she gets what she wants."

"I know," Orion replied, his gaze fixed on the dancing flames. "But so will I. The secrets of the Sapphire Sea Monastery are key to understanding my powers and my past. I won't let Maelstrom or anyone else stand in my way."

As the fire burned low and the crew settled for the night, Orion lay awake, his mind racing with thoughts of the coming challenges. The island was a crucible, and he knew that before his quest was over, he would be tested in ways he could never have imagined. But he was ready. Ready to dance with danger, to embrace his destiny, and to uncover the truths hidden within the Sapphire Sea.

Chapter 5

After the skirmish with Captain Maelstrom's pirates, Orion Nightshade and his crew resumed their quest for the Sapphire Sea Monastery with renewed determination. Guided by the enigmatic map, they ventured deeper into the island's heart, where the dense jungle gave way to a cliff overlooking the vast ocean.

"The map points to something beneath these waters," Orion said, studying the ancient parchment. The markings were cryptic, suggesting a hidden treasure or artifact submerged in the depths below.

Eris, peering over the edge of the cliff, frowned. "The sea can be treacherous, Orion. Are you sure it's down there?"

Orion's eyes were fixed on the churning waves below. "There's only one way to find out."

They set up a makeshift camp by the cliffside. As night fell, Orion sat by the fire, his thoughts as tumultuous as the ocean waves. He remembered Sage Aelius's words about the island holding both secrets and answers. Was he ready for what lay beneath those waves?

The next morning, armed with rudimentary diving gear, Orion and a few brave crew members descended into the sapphire depths. The underwater world was a realm of breathtaking beauty, teeming with vibrant coral and curious fish that darted among the rocks.

As they dove deeper, the light from the surface began to fade, casting eerie shadows on the ocean floor. Orion's amulet pulsed softly, its glow a comforting presence in the dark waters.

They searched tirelessly, navigating through underwater caverns and coral mazes, but the supposed location of the artifact remained elusive. Doubt crept into Orion's mind. Was the map nothing but a clever deception, a wild goose chase meant to lead them astray?

His thoughts were interrupted by a sudden movement in the shadows. A school of luminescent fish swam past, their bodies glowing with an otherworldly light. They seemed to be guiding him, leading him away from the mapped route.

Orion followed, driven by an instinct he couldn't explain. The fish led them to a hidden cave, its entrance barely visible among the sea vines. Inside, they discovered an ancient, water-filled chamber. The walls were adorned with carvings and paintings that depicted scenes of the island's history and the monastery.

Eris swam up to him, her eyes wide with wonder. "Orion, this place... it's like a hidden archive, a record of the island's past."

Orion nodded, his heart racing. The chamber was a treasure trove of knowledge, but there was no sign of the artifact they sought. The realization hit him hard. The map had been a red herring, a distraction meant to lead them away from the real prize.

They resurfaced, the weight of disappointment heavy upon them. Back at the camp, Orion examined the map again, a mix of frustration and resolve in his eyes.

"We've been misled," he announced to his crew. "The true secret of the Sapphire Sea isn't beneath the waves. It's within the monastery itself."

"But how do we find it?" a crew member asked, his voice tinged with exhaustion.

Orion looked out at the ocean, his gaze steely. "We go back to the island's heart. We search every inch if we must. The monastery is here, hiding in plain sight. And with it, the answers we seek."

The crew nodded, their spirits reignited by Orion's determination. They broke camp, ready to embark on the next phase of their journey.

As they trekked back into the island's dense interior, Orion couldn't shake off the feeling of being watched. He remembered the Shadowed Observer, the mysterious figure who had been tracking their movements. Whoever it was, they were a part of this puzzle, another piece in the intricate tapestry of the island's secrets.

That night, under a canopy of stars, Orion lay awake, his mind a whirlwind of thoughts. The island was more than a geographical location; it was a living entity, its spirit intertwined with his destiny.

Eris joined him, her expression thoughtful. "We'll find the monastery, Orion. And with it, the truth about your mother, your magic, and this island."

Orion looked up at the stars, a sense of destiny filling him. "Yes, we will. The Sapphire Sea holds many secrets, but I'm no longer just a seeker. I'm a guardian of its legacy, and I will uncover the truth, no matter what lies ahead."

With the ocean's whispers as their lullaby, Orion and his crew rested, preparing for the challenges that awaited them in their quest to unravel the mysteries of the Sapphire Sea Monastery and the legacy that bound Orion to this enchanted island.

Chapter 6

In the heart of the dense jungle, Orion Nightshade and his crew continued their relentless search for the Sapphire Sea Monastery. The deceptive map had led them astray, but Orion's resolve remained unshaken. The island's mysteries were slowly unraveling, revealing a connection between his shadow magic and the water that seemed to pervade every aspect of this mystical place.

As they trekked through the dense undergrowth, Orion felt a subtle change in the air. The shadows around him seemed more alive, almost responsive to his presence. He could sense the water in the air, in the plants, and in the earth beneath his feet. His shadow magic was evolving, becoming an intricate dance of darkness and fluidity.

Eris, who had been observing Orion closely, spoke up. "Your powers, they're changing. It's like the island itself is teaching you."

Orion nodded, feeling the weight of her words. "The Sapphire Sea and the shadows are becoming one within me. I feel a deeper connection to this place than I ever thought possible."

Their journey led them to a secluded glade where a serene pond lay, its waters crystal clear. As Orion approached, the water's surface rippled, reacting to his presence. He reached out, touching the water, and to his astonishment, the ripples turned into small waves, echoing the movement of his hand.

"It's responding to you," a crew member exclaimed, his voice a mix of awe and disbelief.

Orion was mesmerized. The fusion of his shadow magic with water was something he had never experienced before. He felt an inexplicable bond with the pond, as if it held answers to questions he hadn't yet asked.

As night fell, the crew set up camp by the pond. Orion sat by the water's edge, lost in thought. The moon's reflection on the pond seemed to dance with the shadows, creating a mesmerizing spectacle.

It was then that he noticed it — a figure watching them from the treeline. The Shadowed Observer. Orion had sensed someone tracking them since they arrived on the island, but this was the first time the mysterious figure had shown themselves.

Without a word, Orion stood and slowly approached the figure. As he neared, the shadows seemed to envelop the observer, cloaking their identity.

"Who are you? Why are you following us?" Orion asked, his voice calm but authoritative.

The figure stepped forward, the shadows receding. A man, not much older than Orion, with piercing eyes that reflected a depth of knowledge and understanding. "I am Arlen," he said, his voice steady. "I've been watching you, Orion Nightshade. Your journey, your quest for the monastery, it's no coincidence."

Orion studied Arlen carefully. "What do you mean?"

Arlen glanced at the pond and then back at Orion. "This island, it chooses who it reveals its secrets to. Your connection to the shadows and the water, it's no accident. You are part of a larger destiny, one that is intertwined with the Sapphire Sea Monastery."

Orion's mind raced with questions. "And you? How do you fit into all this?"

"I am a guardian of sorts, a watcher of the island's mysteries. I've seen many come and go, but you, Orion, you are different. You have the potential to unlock the true power of the monastery," Arlen replied, his gaze never wavering.

Orion felt a surge of both excitement and apprehension. The monastery's secrets were within his reach, but so was a responsibility he had only begun to comprehend.

Arlen continued, "But be wary. The path to the monastery is fraught with peril, and not all is as it seems. Trust in your powers, in the bond you've formed with the island."

As Arlen melted back into the shadows, Orion returned to the camp, his mind swirling with the revelations of the night. The connection between his shadow magic and the island's water elements was more profound than he had realized. It was a symbiosis, a fusion of powers that could be the key to unlocking the monastery's secrets.

Eris approached him, concern etched on her face. "What did he say?"

Orion looked at her, a newfound determination in his eyes. "Our journey is more than a quest for answers. It's a destiny that's been waiting for me. We must find the monastery, not just for the secrets it holds, but to fulfill a destiny that's tied to the very essence of this island."

With the moon high in the sky and the pond's waters whispering secrets only he could understand, Orion Nightshade prepared for the next phase of his journey, aware that the path ahead was intertwined with the fate of the Sapphire Sea and the shadows that had become a part of his very soul.

Chapter 7

After days of relentless searching through the dense jungles and veiled paths of the island, Orion Nightshade and his crew finally stumbled upon a hidden trail, overgrown and easily missed. It was Arlen, the Shadowed Observer, who had silently appeared and pointed them towards this forgotten path before vanishing again into the shadows.

The trail wound through the thick foliage, leading them to a part of the island untouched by time. The air was heavy with a sense of ancient magic. The path ended abruptly at the base of a towering cliff, its surface smooth and seemingly insurmountable.

"It's a dead end," Eris said, her voice tinged with frustration. "We've come all this way for nothing."

Orion, however, was not so quick to give up. He approached the cliff, his hand brushing against the cool stone. To his surprise, the amulet around his neck began to glow, its light illuminating intricate carvings on the cliff's surface. They were symbols of water and shadow, intertwining in a complex pattern.

"The monastery," Orion whispered, realization dawning on him. "It's not on the island. It's part of the island."

He focused his energy, channeling his newly evolved powers towards the cliff. The symbols began to glow, responding to his magic. A low rumble echoed through the air as part of the cliff face slid away, revealing a hidden entrance.

The crew entered, finding themselves in a vast chamber. The architecture was ancient, the walls adorned with more symbols and carvings that told the history of the monastery and its connection to the island.

"This is it," Orion said, his voice filled with awe. "The Sapphire Sea Monastery."

They explored the monastery, discovering that it was a labyrinth of chambers and corridors, each revealing more about the history of the place and its guardians. In one room, they found a series of murals depicting the monastery's monks manipulating water with their magic, confirming Sage Aelius's stories.

In the heart of the monastery, they came across a grand hall, where a group of figures robed in blue and green awaited them. The monks of the Sapphire Sea Monastery. The head monk, a man of advanced age with kind eyes, stepped forward.

"Welcome, Orion Nightshade," he said. "We have been expecting you."

"You knew I was coming?" Orion asked, taken aback.

"Yes," the head monk replied. "Your arrival was foretold long ago. You are the one who will unite the powers of shadow and water. You are the key to our monastery's future."

Orion felt a surge of responsibility and purpose. He was here not just to uncover the secrets of his past, but to play a role in the future of the Sapphire Sea Monastery.

The monks led Orion and his crew through the hall, revealing the inner sanctum of the monastery. Here, a serene pool of water reflected the soft light of the chamber. The head monk explained that this pool was the source of their power, a sacred place where the essence of water was strongest.

Orion approached the pool, feeling a deep connection to the water. As he touched its surface, the water responded, swirling around his fingers, merging with the shadows that he commanded.

"It's as we have foreseen," the head monk said, his voice filled with emotion. "You have brought balance to the elements within you. You are ready to learn the true secrets of the Sapphire Sea."

Orion turned to face his crew, a determined look in his eyes. "We have found what we came for. The monastery's secrets are within our grasp. But I sense this is only the beginning of our journey."

The crew nodded, their expressions a mix of awe and loyalty. They had followed Orion into the unknown, and they would continue to stand by him, wherever his quest would lead.

As they prepared to dive deeper into the mysteries of the monastery, Orion felt a sense of fulfillment. He was on the path to discovering not just the secrets of the Sapphire Sea, but also the truth about his own heritage and destiny. The monastery had been revealed, and with it, a new chapter in Orion Nightshade's legacy had begun.

Chapter 8

Within the ancient walls of the Sapphire Sea Monastery, Orion Nightshade and his crew embarked on a journey of discovery, led by Brother Caelum, a monk deeply versed in the monastery's history and secrets. The monastery, a labyrinth of corridors and chambers, was a repository of knowledge and ancient magic. Each room unveiled more about the mystical place, deepening Orion's understanding of his connection to it.

Brother Caelum guided them to a secluded chamber, where a large, intricately carved table held a detailed model of the island and the monastery. The model was a puzzle, each piece a riddle waiting to be solved.

"This," Brother Caelum began, his voice echoing slightly in the chamber, "is the key to finding the true artifact of the Sapphire Sea. Legends speak of its power to control the very essence of water."

Orion leaned over the table, studying the model closely. "But we were led to believe the artifact was hidden underwater."

"A common misconception," Brother Caelum replied. "The true artifact has always been here, within the walls of the monastery. But finding it requires understanding the secrets that this model holds."

The crew set to work, deciphering the clues hidden within the model. It was a task that required both intellect and intuition. As they progressed, pieces of the model moved, revealing hidden compartments and pathways within the monastery.

Orion, with his heightened connection to the monastery's essence, felt a pull towards a specific chamber depicted in the model. "There," he said, pointing. "We need to go there."

Following the newly revealed path, they arrived at a chamber with walls adorned with murals depicting the monastery's history. In the center of the room stood a pedestal with a hollow, shaped perfectly to fit the amulet around Orion's neck.

Without hesitation, Orion placed his amulet into the hollow. The room trembled slightly as hidden mechanisms within the walls activated, revealing a concealed passage.

The passage led them to an underground chamber, where a crystalline artifact pulsed with a soft, blue light. It was suspended above a pool of water, its surface mirroring the artifact's glow.

"This is it," Orion breathed. "The artifact of the Sapphire Sea."

Brother Caelum nodded. "Yes, but it is more than a mere object. It is a conduit of power, a link between the monastery and the island's heart. It can amplify your abilities, but only if you are ready to wield such power."

Orion approached the artifact, his hand hovering over its surface. He could feel the energy coursing through it, resonating with the amulet and his own magic. Closing his eyes, he reached out, touching the artifact.

Instantly, a surge of energy flowed through him, a harmonious blend of shadow and water. The chamber lit up with an ethereal light, and the water in the pool began to rise, forming intricate patterns in the air.

The crew watched in awe as Orion mastered the artifact's power, bending the water to his will. It was a display of magic unlike any they had ever seen.

After a moment, Orion withdrew his hand, the room returning to its former state. He looked at Brother Caelum, a sense of understanding in his eyes.

"I am ready," he said, a newfound confidence in his voice. "I understand my purpose now. The monastery's secrets are not just to be guarded, but to be used for the greater good."

Brother Caelum smiled, a look of pride on his face. "You have indeed proven yourself, Orion Nightshade. The monastery's legacy is safe in your hands."

As they made their way back to the surface, Orion felt a deep sense of fulfillment. He had uncovered the truth about the artifact, but more importantly, he had discovered a deeper purpose. His journey to the Sapphire Sea Monastery had revealed his destiny – to wield the combined powers of shadow and water, to protect the island and its secrets.

But Orion knew that their journey was far from over. Captain Maelstrom and her pirates were still a threat, and the island held more mysteries yet to be uncovered. As they prepared for the challenges ahead, Orion and his crew were united in their resolve to protect the Sapphire Sea Monastery and its ancient legacy.

Chapter 9

In the heart of the Sapphire Sea Monastery, Orion Nightshade's journey took a deeper, more personal turn. Guided by Brother Caelum, he traversed the ancient corridors, each step bringing him closer to the truths about his past and the depths of his magical heritage.

The monastery, with its blend of shadows and water, resonated with Orion's spirit. He felt an ever-growing connection to the place, as if the walls themselves were whispering secrets long forgotten.

"Your mother," Brother Caelum began, breaking the silence as they walked, "she was one of us, a guardian of the Sapphire Sea's secrets. Her legacy lives within these walls, and now, within you."

Orion felt a surge of emotion. "My mother was a part of this place?"

"Yes," Brother Caelum replied solemnly. "She possessed a rare affinity for water magic. Her dedication to protecting the monastery's secrets was unparalleled."

They arrived at a secluded chamber, its walls adorned with intricate carvings depicting the island's history. Brother Caelum gestured towards a mural showing a woman who bore a striking resemblance to Orion.

"This was your mother," he said, his voice filled with reverence. "Her name was Seraphina. She was a protector of the Sapphire Sea, just as you are becoming."

Orion studied the mural, his heart heavy with the weight of newfound knowledge. He had always felt a connection to the water, a pull towards the shadows, but now he understood why. It was his heritage, his birthright.

As they continued their exploration, Brother Caelum revealed more about the monastery's history and the role Orion's mother had played. She had been instrumental in safeguarding a powerful artifact, one that could control the very essence of water.

"Your mother left something for you," Brother Caelum said, leading Orion to a hidden alcove. Inside lay a small chest, intricately carved and sealed with ancient symbols.

Orion opened the chest with a sense of trepidation. Inside, he found a set of scrolls and a pendant, similar to his amulet but imbued with a different energy – one that resonated with the power of water.

"These scrolls," Brother Caelum explained, "contain knowledge passed down through generations. And this pendant, it was your mother's. Together with your amulet, it will help you harness both shadow and water."

Orion felt a profound sense of destiny as he held the pendant. It was as if he was holding a part of his mother, a link to a past he had never known.

As the night fell, Orion sat alone in the chamber, poring over the scrolls. They spoke of the balance between light and dark, the intertwining of fate and magic. He realized that his journey was not just about discovering the monastery's secrets; it was about understanding himself.

The next morning, Orion stood before the monks, his resolve stronger than ever. "I am ready to embrace my destiny," he declared. "I will protect the Sapphire Sea and its secrets, as my mother did before me."

The monks nodded in approval, recognizing the determination in Orion's eyes. He had accepted his legacy, ready to face whatever challenges lay ahead.

As Orion and his crew prepared to leave the monastery, Brother Caelum approached him. "Remember, Orion, the balance of power is delicate. Use your gifts wisely, for the fate of the Sapphire Sea rests in your hands."

Orion clasped the pendant around his neck, feeling the power of both shadow and water coursing through him. "I understand," he said. "And I will not fail."

With a newfound sense of purpose, Orion Nightshade left the Sapphire Sea Monastery, ready to confront the challenges ahead. He had uncovered the secrets of his heritage and embraced his destiny as a guardian of the Sapphire Sea. The journey had transformed him, forging him into a protector of the balance between shadow and water, between past and future.

Chapter 10

The island, once a haven of mystical secrets and quiet solitude, now echoed with the clamor of impending conflict. Orion Nightshade, with the newfound mastery of his shadow and water magic, stood at the forefront, ready to face the pirate marauders led by Captain Leandra Maelstrom. The crew of the Sapphire Sea Monastery, once peaceful guardians of ancient secrets, now prepared to defend their sanctuary.

The pirates, drawn by the allure of power that the monastery was rumored to hold, descended upon the island with a ferocity that matched the crashing waves. Captain Maelstrom, her eyes burning with a mixture of greed and a personal vendetta against Orion, led the charge.

Orion, flanked by his loyal crew and the monastery's monks, faced the marauders. The air was thick with tension, the impending battle a clash of wills and powers.

"You will not defile this sacred place with your greed," Orion declared, his voice resonating with the power of his heritage.

Captain Maelstrom laughed coldly. "I care not for your sacred grounds, Nightshade. The power of the Sapphire Sea will be mine."

The battle erupted with the ferocity of a storm. Orion, channeling his shadow magic, melded with the water's essence, creating waves and torrents that crashed against the pirates. The monks, skilled in their water-based magic, aided him, their spells weaving seamlessly with Orion's shadowy tendrils.

Captain Maelstrom, undeterred, fought with the cunning and brutality that had made her feared across the seas. Her crew, equally ruthless, clashed with Orion's forces, but the synergy of shadow and water magic was overwhelming.

In the midst of the chaos, Orion and Maelstrom found themselves face to face. Their duel was a dance of fury and skill, a testament to their strength and resolve. Orion, empowered by his connection to the monastery and his mother's legacy, matched Maelstrom's every move.

"You fight in vain, Nightshade," Maelstrom sneered, parrying a surge of shadowy water.

Orion, his resolve unwavering, replied, "I fight for something greater than myself. For the legacy of my mother and the protection of this sacred place."

The battle reached its crescendo, with Orion and Maelstrom locked in combat. In a decisive moment, Orion channeled the full extent of his powers, his amulet glowing with an intense light. Shadows and water converged, creating a massive wave that engulfed Maelstrom, breaking her resolve and sweeping her forces back.

Defeated and realizing the futility of her quest, Captain Maelstrom sounded the retreat. Her ship disappeared into the horizon, leaving behind a battered but victorious Orion and his allies.

The aftermath of the battle was a time for healing and reflection. The monastery had been defended, its secrets safe once more. The monks, grateful for Orion's bravery and power, acknowledged him as the true guardian of the Sapphire Sea.

As Orion stood on the shores, watching the sunset paint the sky in hues of gold and crimson, he felt a deep sense of accomplishment. He had protected the monastery, upheld his mother's legacy, and discovered the true extent of his abilities.

Eris approached him, her eyes reflecting the fading light. "You did it, Orion. You've protected the Sapphire Sea and all it stands for."

Orion nodded, his gaze still fixed on the horizon. "Yes, but this is not the end. Captain Maelstrom will return, and there are still mysteries within the monastery that I must uncover."

He turned to face his crew, a determined look in his eyes. "Our journey continues. We must remain vigilant, for the Sapphire Sea holds secrets that we have yet to discover. And I sense that my destiny is still unfolding."

As the night descended upon the island, Orion Nightshade stood tall, a guardian of shadow and water, ready to face whatever challenges lay ahead. The Tides of Confrontation had been weathered, but the journey of Orion's Legacy was far from over.

Chapter 11

In the aftermath of the great confrontation, the Sapphire Sea Monastery returned to its serene state, its ancient walls echoing with the whispers of history and magic. Orion Nightshade stood at the edge of the water, his eyes reflecting the tranquil azure of the sea. The victory against Captain Maelstrom's marauders had not only safeguarded the monastery but also deepened Orion's understanding of his own powers and heritage.

As the sun dipped below the horizon, painting the sky in shades of orange and purple, Orion felt a profound connection with the island and the sea. The monastery's monks, now emerging from their protective seclusion, joined him in silent acknowledgment of his role as their protector.

Brother Caelum approached Orion, his expression one of deep respect. "Orion Nightshade, your bravery and mastery of the elements have saved us all. The monastery is in your debt."

Orion turned to him, a faint smile gracing his lips. "I did what I had to do, Brother Caelum. This place, its secrets, they are part of my legacy now."

The monks gathered around, their faces illuminated by the soft glow of twilight. They spoke of the monastery's history, the water magic that flowed through its halls, and the deep spiritual connection that tied it to the island.

As the night fell, Orion sat with the monks, listening to the tales of the Sapphire Sea, feeling the weight of his responsibility. The night was filled with reflection and revelation, as Orion pondered the whispers of the water, the gentle sound carrying the wisdom of ages.

Suddenly, a soft glow emanated from the center of the monastery, drawing everyone's attention. The monks led Orion to a secluded chamber where a pool of water shimmered under the moonlight. The water was clear and deep, and within it, Orion saw visions of his past adventures and glimpses of what was yet to come.

"The water speaks to you, Orion," Sage Aelius said, his voice filled with awe. "It shows you the path you've walked and the path you're destined to tread."

Orion watched the visions, his heart heavy with the realization of the journey that still lay ahead. He saw images of distant lands, unknown challenges, and faces he had yet to meet. The visions were cryptic, yet they filled Orion with a sense of purpose.

As the visions faded, a soft voice echoed through the chamber. It was the Island's Spirit, its presence soothing and powerful. "Orion Nightshade, you have embraced your destiny. The path you choose will shape not only your future but the fate of the mystical elements you are connected to."

Orion stood up, his resolve strengthened. "I understand. My journey is far from over. There are mysteries to unravel and challenges to face. But I am ready."

The monks nodded in agreement, their expressions filled with admiration and gratitude.

The following morning, Orion prepared to depart from the island. The monks gathered to bid him farewell, their faces a mixture of sadness and hope. Brother Caelum handed Orion a small vial filled with water from the sacred pool. "Take this with you, Orion. Let it be a reminder of your connection to the Sapphire Sea and the strength it bestows upon you."

Orion accepted the vial, feeling its cool weight in his hand. "Thank you, Brother Caelum. I will cherish this gift and the lessons I have learned here."

As Orion's ship set sail, he looked back at the island, its silhouette fading into the distance. He felt a renewed sense of purpose and determination. The whispers in the water had spoken, and he was ready to follow their call.

The Sapphire Sea lay behind him, but his adventure was far from over. Orion Nightshade's legacy was still being written, and the whispers of the water would guide him to his next quest.

Chapter 12

Orion Nightshade stood at the bow of his ship, gazing into the horizon where the sky and sea merged into a boundless expanse. The Sapphire Sea Monastery, now a silhouette in the distance, had become a part of him – a chapter in his life that would forever resonate within his soul.

As the cool sea breeze caressed his face, he reflected on the journey that had brought him to this moment. He had faced formidable adversaries, unraveled ancient secrets, and discovered facets of his magic that he had never known. The revelations about his mother and the monastery had added layers to his identity, deepening his understanding of his place in the world.

Lost in thought, Orion was startled by the approach of a crew member. "Captain Nightshade, we are on course. Where do we head next?" asked the sailor, his voice filled with respect and curiosity.

Orion turned, his dark eyes reflecting the wisdom gained from his recent experiences. "East," he replied confidently. "There are whispers of a land where the sun first greets the sea, a place where shadows dance in the light of dawn. Our adventure takes us there."

The sailor nodded, understanding the depth of Orion's quest. As the crew set to work, adjusting the sails and plotting the course, Orion returned to his contemplation.

The shadowed observer, whose presence had been a constant during his time on the island, remained a mystery. Yet, Orion felt a strange connection to this enigmatic figure, as if their paths were intertwined by fate. He pondered over their identity and the role they might play in his future quests.

As night fell, Orion stood under the stars, the ancient amulet around his neck glowing softly. He felt a surge of power within him, a harmonious blend of shadow and water magic. The transformation that had begun at the monastery was now complete, marking the evolution of his abilities.

His thoughts turned to Captain Leandra Maelstrom, the formidable adversary whose own journey was as enigmatic as it was dangerous. Their paths would undoubtedly cross again, and when they did, Orion would be ready.

Lost in these reflections, a soft, ethereal voice whispered in the wind. It was the Island's Spirit, its presence both comforting and inspiring. "Your journey is far from over, Orion Nightshade. The shadows you cast forward are not just yours alone. They are the echoes of your past and the light of your future."

Orion closed his eyes, embracing the truth in those words. He realized that his journey was more than a quest for adventure; it was a journey of self-discovery, of understanding the intricate tapestry of fate and magic.

As the ship sailed forward, Orion knew that the lessons learned at the Sapphire Sea Monastery would guide him in the days to come. He was no longer just an adventurer; he was a guardian of secrets, a master of the elements, and a seeker of truths hidden in the shadows and the light.

The night deepened, and Orion remained on deck, his gaze fixed on the stars. He was ready for whatever lay ahead, armed with the knowledge and power he had acquired. The Sapphire Sea may have been behind him, but the legacy of its mysteries would forever be a part of him.

In the quiet of the night, Orion Nightshade, the enigmatic hero of the Sapphire Sea, set his course towards new horizons, ready to embrace the adventures that awaited him, wherever they might lead. His story was far from over; in fact, it was just beginning.

The Obsidian Sky

Chapter 1

Orion Nightshade gazed up at the looming silhouette of the floating monastery, his eyes tracing the swirling mists of the Obsidian Cloud encircling it. The air was crisp and biting at this altitude, a stark contrast to the warmth of the valleys below. He adjusted his cloak, feeling the familiar weight of the ancient amulet against his chest. It was a symbol of his lineage, a constant reminder of the legacy he bore.

"Are you certain about this, Orion?" Elder Zephyrus's voice was tinged with concern. The wise leader of the sky monks stood beside him, his long silver hair fluttering in the mountain breeze.

Orion's gaze didn't waver. "I've never been more certain of anything, Elder. The secrets of my family, my very heritage, lie within those walls."

Elder Zephyrus nodded, understanding the depth of Orion's quest. "The Obsidian Cloud is not just a barrier; it's a guardian. Many have tried to breach it and failed. You must be prepared."

Orion turned to him, his dark eyes resolute. "I am. The cloud may hide the monastery, but it also reveals the truth. I must find it."

As they spoke, a shadow passed overhead. Aria Windwhisper, a skilled sky monk and Orion's ally, descended gracefully from the skies. Her long hair flowed around her like a cascade of light, and her eyes sparkled with the wisdom of the winds.

"The assassins are growing bolder, Orion," she warned, landing softly. "We've spotted several near the cloud's perimeter. They're searching for you."

Orion's jaw clenched. The Shadowed One and his aerial assassins had been a thorn in his side for too long. "Let them come. I've evaded them before."

Elder Zephyrus placed a reassuring hand on Orion's shoulder. "You're not alone in this. We, the sky monks, are with you. Your family's legacy with the monastery is deep-rooted."

The group moved towards the edge of the cliff, where the Obsidian Cloud swirled menacingly. Orion took a deep breath, feeling the cool air fill his lungs. This was it—the beginning of his ascent, both literal and metaphorical.

"Remember," Elder Zephyrus said softly, "the cloud reflects your inner self. Face it with a clear heart."

Orion nodded and stepped forward, his cloak billowing behind him. He closed his eyes, focusing on the energy of the amulet. A surge of power coursed through him, and he felt his body lighten.

Opening his eyes, Orion stepped into the Obsidian Cloud. The world around him turned a deep, velvety black, the cloud embracing him like a living entity. He moved with purpose, each step guided by instinct and the subtle pull of the amulet.

As he ascended, images flashed before his eyes—whispers of his family's past, their connection to the monastery, the pact made centuries ago. The cloud was testing him, challenging his resolve.

Suddenly, a figure emerged from the darkness—an aerial assassin, poised to strike. Orion reacted instantly, his body moving with the grace and precision of a predator. The assassin lunged, but Orion was faster. He parried and struck, his movements a blur in the obsidian shroud.

More assassins appeared, but Orion was undeterred. He fought with a combination of stealth, agility, and the sharp tactical acumen that had become his trademark. Each enemy that fell only strengthened his resolve.

Finally, the cloud began to thin, and the floating monastery came into view—a majestic structure of ancient stone and ethereal beauty. Orion stepped onto the solid ground of the monastery, his heart pounding with exhilaration and anticipation.

He turned to see Aria and Elder Zephyrus emerging from the cloud, their expressions a mix of relief and pride.

"You've passed the first test, Orion," Elder Zephyrus said, his blue eyes shining with admiration.

Orion looked up at the towering monastery, feeling a deep connection to this place and his ancestors. "The journey has just begun," he murmured. "I'm ready to uncover the truths hidden within these walls."

And with that, Orion Nightshade, the enigmatic adventurer, took his first step into the heart of the floating monastery, ready to unravel the mysteries of the Obsidian Cloud and his family's legacy. The adventure, fraught with danger and discovery, was just beginning.

Chapter 2

The ancient stones of the floating monastery whispered secrets of ages past as Orion Nightshade stepped through its archaic halls. The air was thick with the scent of old parchment and burning incense, a sensory tapestry that seemed to transport him back in time. He trailed his fingers along the walls, feeling the pulse of history in every crevice.

Elder Zephyrus guided him, his silver hair almost glowing in the dim light. "This monastery has stood for centuries, Orion. It is a sanctuary for those who seek knowledge of the skies and beyond."

Orion's eyes absorbed every detail, from the ornate tapestries depicting celestial battles to the serene statues of past sky monks. "And my family," he said, "they were a part of this?"

"Yes," Elder Zephyrus replied, leading him into a vast chamber adorned with intricate murals. "Your ancestors were instrumental in the construction of this sanctuary. They understood the balance between the earth and the sky."

Aria Windwhisper joined them, her presence as light as the breeze. "Your family's legacy is interwoven with the very essence of this place, Orion."

Orion turned to her, a flicker of curiosity in his dark eyes. "How so?"

Elder Zephyrus gestured towards a mural, depicting a figure cloaked in shadows, standing beside a monk under a star-filled sky. "Centuries ago, your ancestor made a pact with the sky monks. It was an alliance that helped maintain the equilibrium between the magical forces."

Orion studied the mural, feeling a connection to the shadowed figure. "And what of the Obsidian Cloud? What role does it play?"

Master Callum, a scholarly monk with keen eyes, stepped forward. "The Obsidian Cloud is not just a natural phenomenon. It's a manifestation of ancient magic, a protective shield for the monastery. It possesses the ability to manipulate air, a power your family was deeply involved in harnessing."

Orion's gaze drifted to the cloud visible through a high window. "Manipulate air?" he echoed, a sense of wonder in his tone.

"Yes," Aria chimed in. "The monks here have mastered the art of air manipulation, using it for protection, healing, and sometimes, in the darker times, for combat."

The weight of history pressed upon Orion as he absorbed this information. The connection between his family and the monastery was more profound than he had imagined.

As they ventured deeper into the monastery, they came across Vayla, a young novice monk with bright eyes and an eager smile. "Orion Nightshade," she said, her voice tinged with excitement. "I've read about your family. It's an honor to meet you."

Orion offered a small smile. "The honor is mine, Vayla. Your knowledge of my family..."

Vayla's eyes sparkled. "Oh, the texts here speak volumes! Your ancestor was revered for his wisdom and courage. He was a true ally to the monks."

Their journey took them to a secluded part of the monastery, where ancient texts were preserved. Master Callum gestured towards a dusty tome. "This is where your quest truly begins, Orion. These texts hold the key to understanding the Obsidian Cloud and your family's role in its history."

Orion opened the book, his fingers trembling slightly. The pages were filled with arcane symbols and cryptic writings, speaking of rituals, pacts, and the balance of elemental forces.

Elder Zephyrus observed him. "Remember, Orion, the path of knowledge is fraught with challenges. You must be ready to confront the truths you find."

Orion looked up, determination etching his features. "I've come this far. I'm ready for whatever lies ahead."

As they left the library, a sense of unease settled over the group. The Shadowed One's influence was a constant threat, and the presence of the aerial assassins loomed like a dark cloud.

"The assassins will not rest until they have thwarted your quest," Aria warned, her gaze scanning the skies.

Orion nodded, his hand resting on the amulet around his neck. "Then we must be vigilant. My journey to understand my legacy and the mysteries of the Obsidian Cloud has just begun."

The floating monastery, with its ancient wisdom and mystical aura, had opened a new chapter in Orion's life. A chapter filled with discovery, danger, and the unfolding of a legacy that would redefine his destiny. As the sun set behind the Obsidian Cloud, casting long shadows across the monastery, Orion Nightshade stood resolute, ready to embrace the path that lay before him.

Chapter 3

Within the ancient, hallowed halls of the floating monastery, Orion Nightshade, accompanied by Master Callum, dove into the heart of the secrets that had long eluded him. The chamber, lit by flickering candles, cast long shadows that danced across the walls, mirroring Orion's own restless thoughts.

"The Obsidian Cloud," Master Callum began, his voice echoing slightly in the vast space, "is more than a mere weather phenomenon. It is a living, breathing entity, shaped by the will and magic of those who have mastered its secrets."

Orion, his gaze fixed on an ancient scroll spread before him, nodded slowly. "And my ancestors? They were part of this mastery?"

"Yes, Orion. Your lineage is deeply entwined with the cloud's essence. The Nightshades were not only protectors but also enhancers of its power," Callum explained, his fingers tracing the intricate symbols on the scroll.

Orion absorbed the words, feeling a connection to the cloud that went beyond mere curiosity. "How does it manipulate air?" he inquired, his eyes scanning the ancient texts for answers.

"The monks of this monastery, through intense meditation and practice, learned to commune with the elements. They discovered that the Obsidian Cloud could be attuned to respond to their thoughts, to bend the air to their will," Callum elaborated, his eyes reflecting the flickering candlelight.

Orion's thoughts turned to Aria Windwhisper, her graceful control over the winds during their ascent. "Aria, she has this mastery?"

Callum nodded. "Yes, she is among our most skilled. The air responds to her like an extension of her own being."

The conversation was interrupted by the sudden entrance of Elder Zephyrus, his expression grave. "Orion, we have sensed a disturbance. The Shadowed One's assassins, they are closer than we anticipated."

Orion stood up, his instincts on high alert. "I'm ready to face them."

Elder Zephyrus placed a hand on his shoulder. "Be cautious, Orion. They are not just mere mercenaries; they are skilled in dark arts, possibly trained in the ways of the Obsidian Cloud."

The revelation sent a chill down Orion's spine. If the assassins had knowledge of the cloud, the danger they posed was far greater than he had imagined.

Late that night, Orion stood on a balcony overlooking the cloud-covered valleys below. The air was crisp, and the stars shone brightly, undimmed by the city lights of the world below. He pondered the weight of his heritage, the responsibility of his lineage. The Obsidian Cloud, a symbol of his family's legacy, seemed to beckon him with its swirling mists.

Aria joined him, her presence a silent comfort. "The cloud is restless tonight," she observed, her gaze lost in the undulating mists.

Orion turned to her, his eyes reflecting the starlight. "Aria, if the assassins have knowledge of the cloud, how can we stop them?"

Aria's expression was thoughtful. "The cloud is ancient, Orion. It has secrets that even we, the sky monks, have yet to fully understand. But one thing is certain — it responds to the purity of intent. Your heart, your quest for truth, is your greatest weapon against them."

The words resonated within Orion, igniting a newfound determination. "Then I will face them with the truth as my shield," he declared, his voice steady.

The following days were spent in intense study and training. Orion, under the tutelage of Aria and Master Callum, began to grasp the basics of air manipulation. He learned to feel the ebb and flow of the wind, to sense its patterns and whispers.

One evening, as Orion sat deep in meditation, he felt a sudden shift in the air. A cold, malevolent presence seemed to seep through the walls of the monastery. The Shadowed One's assassins had arrived.

Orion rose, his senses heightened. He moved through the corridors, each step silent as a shadow. As he approached the courtyard, he saw them — cloaked figures, moving with lethal grace, their eyes glinting with malice.

Without hesitation, Orion engaged them. His training with the monks had honed his agility, and he moved like the wind itself, swift and unpredictable. The assassins were skilled, but Orion was driven by a deeper purpose.

As he fought, he felt a connection to the air around him, a sense of unity with the elements. He used this newfound power to his advantage, manipulating the air to disorient and outmaneuver his opponents.

The battle raged, a dance of shadows and wind, until the last of the assassins lay defeated at his feet. Orion stood, his chest heaving, the adrenaline still coursing through his veins.

Elder Zephyrus and Aria arrived, their expressions a mix

of relief and awe. "You have done well, Orion," Zephyrus said, pride evident in his voice.

Orion looked up at the Obsidian Cloud, now calm and serene. "The secrets of the sky are deep and vast. I have much to learn, but I am ready for the journey ahead."

With the defeat of the assassins, Orion's resolve strengthened. The monastery, with its ancient wisdom and mystical air, had become a sanctuary and a training ground for him. He knew that the path ahead was fraught with peril, but he was no longer just an adventurer seeking answers; he was a guardian of a legacy, a protector of the secrets of the sky.

Chapter 4

In the aftermath of his first confrontation with the aerial assassins, Orion Nightshade found himself in a state of heightened vigilance. The floating monastery, once a haven of peace and learning, now seemed to echo with unseen threats. The night sky, previously a canvas of starlit beauty, now served as a reminder of the dangers lurking in the shadows.

Elder Zephyrus, sensing Orion's unease, summoned him to his private chambers. The room was filled with ancient artifacts and scrolls, each holding secrets of the past. The elder's blue eyes, wise and deep, met Orion's with a steady gaze.

"Orion, the attack was not a mere coincidence. It was a clear message from The Shadowed One," Elder Zephyrus began, his voice calm yet carrying an undercurrent of concern.

Orion nodded, his hands clenched at his sides. "I know. But why? Why now, and why here at the monastery?"

"The monastery holds more than just knowledge of the skies, Orion. It is a bastion of power, a place where the veil between the natural and the supernatural is thin," the elder explained. "Your presence here, coupled with your family's legacy, has undoubtedly drawn attention."

Aria Windwhisper joined the conversation, her face etched with worry. "We have increased our vigilance. The monastery's defenses are strong, but we must not underestimate The Shadowed One's cunning."

Orion felt a surge of frustration. "I came here seeking answers about my family, not to bring danger to your doorstep."

Elder Zephyrus placed a reassuring hand on his shoulder. "You are not to blame, Orion. The forces at play are beyond any of us. But together, we are stronger. Your quest is now intertwined with the fate of this place."

The next day, as Orion walked through the monastery's ancient corridors, he encountered Vayla, the young novice monk. Her youthful energy was a stark contrast to the tension that had gripped the monastery.

"Orion, I've heard about the attack," she said, her eyes wide with a mix of fear and excitement. "Is it true that you fought them off single-handedly?"

Orion managed a small smile. "I had help from the wind."

Vayla's expression turned serious. "I want to help too. I may not be a skilled fighter like Aria, but I know the monastery's secrets. There are hidden passages and rooms that even the elder monks don't frequent."

Intrigued, Orion followed Vayla to a secluded part of the monastery. Hidden behind a tapestry was a narrow passage, leading to a small chamber. The room was filled with dusty tomes and ancient artifacts.

"This was a meeting place for the original pact-makers," Vayla explained, her voice hushed in reverence. "Your ancestors and the first sky monks."

Orion's gaze fell upon a faded mural depicting the signing of a pact, his ancestor's figure prominent among the monks. A sense of connection to his past, both awe-inspiring and burdensome, filled him.

As they explored the chamber, Orion's keen eyes caught a glimpse of something unusual—a small, almost imperceptible marking on the floor. It was a symbol he had seen in the texts about the Obsidian Cloud.

"This symbol," Orion mused aloud, "it's linked to the cloud's deepest secrets."

Vayla leaned in, her curiosity piqued. "Maybe it's a clue to why The Shadowed One is so interested in you and the monastery."

Orion knew she was right. The symbol could be the key to understanding the true nature of the threat they faced.

Later that evening, Orion shared his discovery with Elder Zephyrus and Aria. The elder monk stroked his silver beard thoughtfully. "This symbol represents a convergence of energies, a point where the cloud's power is most potent. It is believed that at such a point, one could wield the cloud's power to a devastating effect."

Aria's expression grew dark. "If The Shadowed One knows of this, then his intentions are far more sinister than we imagined."

Orion stood up, his resolve hardening. "Then we must find this convergence point before he does. We must protect the cloud and its secrets."

The following days were spent in preparation. Orion, Aria, and a select group of monks scoured the ancient texts and explored the hidden recesses of the monastery. They discovered more symbols, each pointing to a location within the monastery grounds.

As they pieced together the puzzle, a chilling realization dawned upon them. The convergence point was located in the heart of the monastery, beneath the central spire.

"It's not just a power source for the cloud," Orion concluded, his mind racing with possibilities and dangers. "It's a weapon, one that could be used to control or destroy the cloud itself."

The gravity of the situation weighed heavily upon them all. The monastery was no longer just a place of learning; it had become the focal point of a struggle that could determine the fate of the Obsidian Cloud and the legacy of the Nightshade family.

Orion knew that the coming confrontation with The Shadowed One would be unlike any he had faced before. It was not just a battle of physical prowess but a fight for the very soul of the legacy he had come to understand and embrace. As the stars twinkled above the shrouded monastery, Orion steeled himself for the shadows and suspicions that lay ahead, ready to defend the legacy that was both his birthright and his burden.

Chapter 5

Orion Nightshade sat in the dimly lit chamber, his eyes fixated on the ancient text sprawled before him. The air in the monastery's library was thick with the scent of old parchment and time-worn leather. Master Callum, ever the patient mentor, stood by his side, deciphering the cryptic language of the text.

"The pact," Callum began in a solemn tone, "was not merely a commitment of mutual aid between your ancestors and the sky monks. It was a binding of fates, a sharing of destinies."

Orion absorbed each word, the weight of history pressing upon his shoulders. "So, my family didn't just help the monks; they became part of the very essence of this place?"

"Precisely," Callum nodded. "The Nightshades pledged to protect the Obsidian Cloud and, in turn, the cloud offered them a part of its power. It's a symbiosis that has lasted centuries."

Orion ran a hand through his jet-black hair, his mind racing. "Then the belief that my family broke the pact..."

"It's a misconception, perhaps propagated by those who feared your family's power or misunderstood the nature of the pact," Callum explained.

At that moment, Elder Zephyrus entered the room, his presence commanding yet comforting. "Orion, the time has come to confront the truth. Your family did not break the pact. They sacrificed greatly to maintain it."

Orion looked up, his deep, dark eyes seeking answers. "What kind of sacrifices?"

"Your ancestors were often the first line of defense against threats to the monastery and the cloud. They used their connection to the cloud to fend off enemies, sometimes at the cost of their own lives," Zephyrus revealed, his voice tinged with respect.

The revelation struck Orion like a thunderbolt. All this time, he had been burdened by a guilt that was not his to bear. His family had not betrayed their oath; they had been its staunchest defenders.

"Why was this hidden from me?" Orion asked, a mix of relief and frustration in his voice.

"It was a measure to protect you," Aria Windwhisper said, entering the chamber. "The truth about the pact and your family's role was kept secret to keep you safe from those who sought to exploit or destroy it."

Orion stood up, his stature commanding yet graceful. "Then the attacks, The Shadowed One's interest in me... it's all connected to the pact."

"Yes," Zephyrus affirmed. "They seek to break what your family has protected for generations."

Orion's gaze turned steely, his resolve hardening. "Then I will continue what my ancestors started. I will protect the monastery and the cloud."

The following days were marked by intense training and research. Orion, guided by Aria and Master Callum, dove deeper into the mysteries of the Obsidian Cloud and the ancient arts practiced by the sky monks. He learned to harness the cloud's power, to feel its ebb and flow like an extension of his being.

But it wasn't just physical training that occupied Orion's time. He spent hours with Vayla, exploring the hidden corners of the monastery, uncovering relics and texts that shed more light on his family's history.

One evening, as Orion and Vayla pored over a tattered scroll, they came across a startling revelation — a prophecy that spoke of a Nightshade who would rise to face a darkness that threatened to engulf both the monastery and the cloud.

"This speaks of you, Orion," Vayla said, her eyes wide with awe. "You're the one the prophecy foretold."

Orion pondered the words, a sense of destiny enveloping him. He was no longer just a seeker of truths; he was a key player in a saga that spanned centuries.

The realization of his role in the ancient pact and the prophecy spurred Orion to take decisive action. He convened a meeting with Elder Zephyrus, Aria, Master Callum, and a few trusted monks.

"We must prepare for what's to come," Orion declared, his voice resonating with authority. "The Shadowed One will not stop until he has unraveled the pact and seized the power of the cloud. We must protect this legacy at all costs."

The monks nodded in agreement, inspired by Orion's leadership and determination.

In the weeks that followed, the monastery became a fortress, bracing for the inevitable confrontation. Orion trained relentlessly, honing his skills and deepening his connection to the cloud.

But it wasn't just physical preparation that occupied Orion's mind. He spent long nights contemplating the legacy he had inherited, the sacrifices his family had made. He realized that his journey was not just about uncovering the past; it was about embracing his role in a story much larger than himself.

As Orion stood on the balcony overlooking the Obsidian Cloud, he felt a sense of peace amidst the brewing storm. He was ready to face the darkness, to defend the legacy of his family and the sacred pact they had upheld.

The chapter closed with Orion, a figure of strength and resolve, gazing into the night, prepared for the battle that lay ahead. He was no longer haunted by doubts about his family's honor; he was empowered by the knowledge of their sacrifice and dedication. The legacy of the Nightshades was in safe hands, and Orion was ready to write the next chapter in its storied history.

Chapter 6

The air was charged with tension at the floating monastery, a silent anticipation hanging like a shroud over its ancient stones. Orion Nightshade, now fully aware of his legacy and the weight it carried, stood on the battlements, his gaze piercing through the swirling mists of the Obsidian Cloud. The time for preparation had passed; the time for action was upon them.

Elder Zephyrus joined him, his presence a steady force amidst the brewing storm. "The assassins will come, Orion. The Shadowed One knows the importance of this night. The convergence is upon us."

Orion nodded, his mind a whirlwind of strategy and resolve. "I am ready, Elder. My ancestors fought to protect this legacy, and I will do the same."

The stillness of the night was suddenly broken by a flurry of movement. Shadows detached themselves from the cloud, taking form as the aerial assassins descended upon the monastery with silent grace and deadly intent.

Orion sprang into action, his body moving with the fluidity and precision that had become his trademark. Aria Windwhisper was by his side, her mastery over the air a vital ally in the battle.

The courtyard became a maelstrom of combat, Orion and Aria at its heart. The assassins were skilled, but they were no match for Orion's newfound prowess and Aria's elemental control.

As they fought, a larger, more ominous figure emerged from the cloud — The Shadowed One. His presence was like a dark cloud, his intent clear and malevolent.

Orion felt a surge of energy course through him, the amulet around his neck pulsating with power. He knew this was the moment, the climax of his journey so far.

The Shadowed One moved with a grace that belied his sinister nature, his attacks a blend of shadow and deception. Orion met him head-on, his own movements a dance of light and shadow.

The battle raged, a symphony of clashing blades and swirling winds. Orion and The Shadowed One were evenly matched, each blow met with a counter, each attack a test of skill and will.

As they fought, Orion realized the true nature of his adversary. The Shadowed One was not just a master assassin; he was a mirror to Orion's own darkness, a manifestation of the shadows he had always sought to understand.

The realization fueled Orion's resolve. He fought not just with his body but with his spirit, his every move an embodiment of the legacy he carried.

The monastery's monks joined the fray, their own skills honed through years of practice. They moved as one with the wind, their chants a powerful force against the assassins.

Vayla, the young novice monk, proved her worth, using her knowledge of the monastery's secrets to outmaneuver the enemy, guiding the defenders to advantageous positions.

The battle reached its zenith as Orion and The Shadowed One stood atop the highest tower, the Obsidian Cloud swirling around them. Their swords clashed, sparks flying, as they fought for control of the monastery's fate.

With a final, mighty effort, Orion disarmed The Shadowed One, sending him plummeting into the cloud below. The battle was won, but the war was far from over.

Orion stood victorious yet introspective, his gaze lost in the depths of the cloud. He had protected the monastery, upheld his family's legacy, but at what cost?

Elder Zephyrus approached, placing a hand on Orion's shoulder. "You have done well, young Nightshade. Your ancestors would be proud."

Orion looked at the elder, a mix of triumph and sorrow in his eyes. "This is just the beginning, isn't it? The Shadowed One was but a harbinger of darker things to come."

"Yes," Zephyrus agreed, his eyes reflecting the wisdom of his years. "But you have shown that you are more than capable of facing whatever lies ahead. The Obsidian Cloud has chosen well."

As dawn broke, casting a golden light over the monastery, Orion realized that his journey was far from over. He had faced his shadows, both literal and metaphorical, and emerged stronger.

But questions remained. The Shadowed One's motives, the true extent of the pact's power, and Orion's role in it all. These were mysteries yet to be unraveled.

Orion Nightshade, the enigmatic warrior with a legacy as deep and mysterious as the Obsidian Cloud itself, stood ready for whatever lay ahead. The battles in the breeze were just the beginning of a journey that would test the very limits of his strength, his will, and his destiny.

Chapter 7

In the aftermath of the fierce battle against The Shadowed One and his minions, Orion Nightshade found himself wandering the quiet corridors of the floating monastery, his thoughts a tumultuous sea. The victory had been significant, but the cost weighed heavily on his heart. The echoes of the past seemed to resonate through the ancient walls, speaking of sacrifices and secrets long buried.

Elder Zephyrus found Orion gazing out over the mist-shrouded valleys from a stone balcony. "Your thoughts are troubled, Orion," he said, his voice a gentle nudge in the silence.

Orion turned, his dark eyes reflecting the turmoil within. "The battle is won, but I feel no peace. My ancestors' sacrifices, the pact, the cloud — it's a legacy that feels like a labyrinth."

Zephyrus joined him at the balcony, his wise eyes surveying the horizon. "Your journey is not just about battles fought in the physical realm. It's a journey into the depths of your lineage, into the heart of the mysteries that surround us."

A sense of determination settled over Orion. "I need to understand more, Elder. I need to explore these mysteries, to uncover the truths my ancestors left behind."

The next day, Orion, accompanied by Vayla and Aria Windwhisper, embarked on a quest to dive deeper into the monastery's history. They explored hidden chambers and forgotten archives, where dust-laden books and ancient artifacts whispered tales of yore.

In a secluded chamber, Vayla uncovered a series of murals depicting the original signing of the pact between the Nightshade family and the sky monks. The images were vibrant, telling a story of unity and a shared destiny.

Orion traced the lines of the mural with a reverent finger. "This is where it all began," he murmured, the weight of history palpable in the air.

Aria, standing beside him, added, "Your family didn't just uphold a pact; they embraced a destiny. They became guardians of a legacy as old as the monastery itself."

Their exploration led them to a hidden crypt beneath the monastery, where the remains of Orion's ancestors lay in eternal rest. The air was thick with the essence of time, each tomb a testament to the sacrifices made by the Nightshade lineage.

Orion felt a deep connection to this sacred place, the final resting ground of his forebears. He knelt before the tombs, a sense of communion with his ancestors filling his soul.

"It's more than a lineage of duty," Orion spoke softly, almost to himself. "It's a lineage of courage, of unwavering commitment to a cause greater than oneself."

As they dove deeper, they discovered a sealed chamber, its entrance marked with the symbol of the Obsidian Cloud. With a sense of trepidation, Orion pushed open the ancient door, revealing a room that seemed untouched by time.

Inside, they found a trove of relics and texts, each piece a fragment of the legacy of the Nightshade family. Among the artifacts lay a scroll, its parchment brittle with age, yet the writing was as clear as if it had been penned yesterday.

Orion carefully unfurled the scroll, his heart pounding with anticipation. The scroll contained a prophecy, one that spoke of a Nightshade who would stand at the crossroads of time, a key to averting a catastrophe that threatened the very essence of the Obsidian Cloud.

"This prophecy," Orion said, his voice laced with awe, "it speaks of events yet to come, of a challenge that I must face."

Aria looked over his shoulder, her eyes scanning the ancient script. "It seems your journey is far from over, Orion. This prophecy is a call to action, a mandate set by your ancestors."

As they returned to the upper levels of the monastery, Orion felt a renewed sense of purpose. The past had spoken, revealing secrets and prophecies that shaped his path forward. He was not just Orion Nightshade, the man; he was Orion Nightshade, the bearer of a legacy that spanned generations.

That night, as he stood once again on the balcony, gazing out at the Obsidian Cloud, Orion felt a deep connection to his ancestors. The echoes of the past had provided clarity and direction, and he knew what he must do.

With the support of Elder Zephyrus, Aria, and Vayla, Orion prepared for the next phase of his journey. He would dive deeper into the mysteries of the Obsidian Cloud, confront the challenges foretold in the prophecy, and uphold the legacy of the Nightshade family.

As the moon cast its silvery glow over the monastery, Orion Nightshade stood resolute, a figure of strength and determination. The echoes of the past had become a clarion call to the future, and he was ready to answer it.

Chapter 8

In the heart of the floating monastery, beneath the ever-shifting veil of the Obsidian Cloud, Orion Nightshade grappled with the enormity of his legacy. Each revelation, each uncovered secret of his family's past, seemed to add another layer to the labyrinthine journey he found himself on. The victory over The Shadowed One and his minions was significant, but it was merely a precursor to the challenges that lay ahead.

Elder Zephyrus, seeing the contemplative figure of Orion staring into the distance, approached him with a serene expression. "The battles you face are not just for the present, Orion. They are a test for the future, a forging of your spirit for what is yet to come."

Orion turned, his eyes reflecting a storm of emotions. "I feel as though I am at a crossroads, Elder. One path leads deeper into the mysteries of my family and the cloud, the other into an unknown future."

"It is the way of the Nightshade," Zephyrus replied. "To embrace the unknown, to find strength in the mysteries of our world. Your journey is a turning point, not just for you, but for all who are connected to the Obsidian Cloud."

In the days that followed, Orion dedicated himself to intense training and study. He dove into the most arcane texts, seeking to understand the full extent of the pact his ancestors had forged and the true nature of the Obsidian Cloud. Aria Windwhisper, ever his ally, aided him, her knowledge of the elemental magic proving invaluable.

During a sparring session, Aria stopped, her gaze intense. "Orion, you have grown stronger, more attuned to the forces around you. But remember, the greatest strength comes from within, from understanding who you are and the path you must take."

Orion nodded, absorbing her words. The physical battles were demanding, but it was the internal struggle, the fight to understand his place in the legacy, that proved the most challenging.

One night, as Orion wandered the ancient halls of the monastery, he came across a hidden chamber, its entrance obscured by a tapestry. Inside, he found a series of murals depicting the history of the Nightshade family and the sky monks. The images were alive with magic, each scene telling a story of sacrifice, power, and destiny.

As Orion studied the murals, a particular image caught his eye. It showed a Nightshade ancestor, standing at the heart of the Obsidian Cloud, his arms raised as if commanding the very essence of the cloud. Orion felt a connection to this image, a sense of familiarity that resonated within his soul.

"This is it," Orion murmured to himself. "The key to understanding my family's bond with the cloud."

He spent hours in the chamber, each mural revealing more of the ancient pact and the responsibilities it entailed. It was clear that his family's bond with the cloud was more profound than he had ever imagined.

Armed with this new knowledge, Orion sought out Elder Zephyrus. "I have seen the murals, Elder. I understand now. My family was not just bound to protect the cloud; they were part of it, integral to its very existence."

Zephyrus nodded, a look of approval in his eyes. "You are beginning to understand, Orion. Your journey is about embracing that bond, about becoming one with the legacy you were born into."

But with understanding came a new sense of foreboding. Orion realized that the threat to the Obsidian Cloud was far from over. The Shadowed One might have been defeated, but the danger to the cloud and the monastery lingered like a shadow at the edge of light.

In a meeting with Aria, Vayla, and a council of sky monks, Orion laid out his plan. "We must strengthen our defenses, dive deeper into the mysteries of the cloud. We must be prepared for whatever comes next."

The monks agreed, each understanding the gravity of the situation. They pledged their support, their skills, and their knowledge to aid Orion in his quest.

As the meeting concluded, Orion stood alone, gazing out at the Obsidian Cloud. He knew that the coming days would test him as never before. The turning point of his journey was upon him, a moment that would define not just his future, but the fate of the cloud and all who relied on its power.

With determination etched on his features, Orion Nightshade prepared for the challenges ahead. The echoes of his ancestors' sacrifices bolstered his resolve, and the weight of his legacy no longer felt like a burden, but a source of strength. The path forward was fraught with uncertainty, but Orion was ready to face it, to embrace his destiny and protect the legacy of the Nightshade family.

Chapter 9

In the serene quietude of the floating monastery, amidst the whispering winds and the shifting shades of the Obsidian Cloud, Orion Nightshade found himself in a state of deep introspection. The recent victories and revelations had brought him to a precipice, both in understanding his family's legacy and in confronting his own inner turmoil.

Elder Zephyrus, sensing the depth of Orion's contemplation, approached him in the monastery's ancient library, where Orion was poring over the texts of his ancestors. "The path of self-discovery is often the most arduous, Orion. It is a journey that tests the spirit as much as the sword," the Elder spoke with a wisdom as ancient as the stones around them.

Orion looked up, his eyes reflecting the storm of his thoughts. "I find myself questioning everything, Elder. My role, my family's past, the very essence of this legacy I bear."

"It is a natural part of embracing your destiny. Doubt and reflection are the crucibles in which true strength is forged," Zephyrus replied.

As Orion dove deeper into the annals of his lineage, he stumbled upon a series of personal journals penned by his ancestors. Each entry revealed not just the history of their battles and the sacrifices made but also their fears, hopes, and the personal cost of their commitments.

One evening, as Orion read a journal entry by his great-grandfather, a passage struck a chord within him. It spoke of the loneliness of the path, the burden of expectations, and the never-ending struggle between light and darkness within one's own soul.

Orion felt a kinship with these words, realizing that his ancestors, too, had grappled with similar doubts and internal conflicts. It gave him a sense of connection, a realization that he was part of a continuum, a legacy that was as much about human struggle as it was about heroism.

Seeking solace and understanding, Orion sought out Aria Windwhisper in the monastery's serene gardens. Under the ethereal glow of the Obsidian Cloud, he shared his turmoil with her.

Aria listened intently, her eyes mirroring the night sky. "The shadows within are often the hardest to confront, Orion. But remember, it is often in the darkest nights that the stars shine the brightest."

Orion pondered her words, finding comfort in their truth. The conversation with Aria became a turning point, helping him to see that his internal struggle was an integral part of his journey, a necessary path to true understanding and acceptance of his role.

In the following days, Orion embraced his training and studies with a newfound perspective. He began to understand that the legacy of the Nightshade family was not just about the physical defense of the monastery or the mastery of the Obsidian Cloud's magic. It was also about the resilience of the spirit, the courage to face one's own shadows.

This realization brought a sense of clarity and purpose to Orion. He started to train the younger monks, sharing not only his skills but also the wisdom he had gained. In doing so, he found a sense of peace and fulfillment, seeing his own struggles and victories reflected in the eyes of his protégés.

Vayla, who had been a constant companion in his journey, approached him one evening with a curious artifact in her hands. "I found this in one of the hidden chambers. It seems to be connected to your family's history."

The artifact was an ancient compass, its needle oscillating wildly before settling in a direction that defied logic. "It points not to the north, but to something else... something hidden," Vayla said with a sense of wonder.

Orion held the compass, feeling a pulsating energy emanating from it. "This may be the key to unlocking another part of my family's legacy, another piece of the puzzle."

As the chapter drew to a close, Orion stood at the edge of the monastery, the compass in his hand pointing towards a new mystery, a new chapter in his journey. He realized that the legacy he carried was not a burden but a beacon, guiding him through the shadows towards a destiny yet to be fulfilled.

The night sky above the monastery was a tapestry of stars and clouds, a mirror to the journey Orion Nightshade was on — a journey not just of battles and magic, but of inner discovery, of embracing the light and the dark within, and of continuing the legacy that had been passed down through generations. A legacy not just of shadows, but of unyielding light.

Chapter 10

The air within the floating monastery was dense with anticipation as Orion Nightshade stood in the central chamber, his gaze fixed on an ancient relic that had been hidden for generations. The artifact, a crystalline sphere, pulsed with a light that seemed to resonate with the very heartbeat of the Obsidian Cloud. This was the moment Orion had been preparing for, the revelation of a truth that would redefine his understanding of his family's legacy.

Elder Zephyrus, alongside Aria Windwhisper and Master Callum, watched in silence. They knew that what was about to unfold would change everything they knew about the pact between the Nightshade family and the sky monks.

Orion reached out, his fingers brushing against the sphere. Instantly, a flood of images and voices filled his mind. He saw his ancestors, not as the betrayers of a sacred pact, but as its most ardent protectors. He witnessed the signing of the pact, the binding of the Nightshade family to the Obsidian Cloud, and the sacrifices they made to keep this bond alive.

The voices spoke of a hidden truth, a secret so profound that it had been shrouded in mystery for centuries. The Nightshades were not just guardians of the cloud; they were part of its very essence. Their magic, their very life force, was intertwined with the cloud, giving them the power to manipulate the air and protect the monastery.

Orion staggered back, overwhelmed by the revelation. Elder Zephyrus stepped forward, his eyes reflecting a mix of sorrow and pride. "You now know the truth, Orion. Your family's legacy is far greater than you imagined. You are not just a protector of the cloud; you are its embodiment."

Aria approached Orion, placing a reassuring hand on his shoulder. "This changes everything, Orion. Your connection to the cloud is not just a duty; it's a part of who you are."

Master Callum, the keeper of the monastery's texts, nodded in agreement. "The Obsidian Cloud is more than just a mystical phenomenon. It's a living entity, and your family has been its caretaker through generations."

Orion, still processing the revelation, looked at the sphere, now dimmed and silent. "I thought I was searching for the truth about my family's betrayal. But instead, I found our true purpose. We were never the breakers of the pact; we were its strongest link."

The realization brought a sense of clarity and purpose to Orion. He now understood why the aerial assassins, led by The Shadowed One, were so intent on destroying him and the monastery. They were not just after power; they were trying to sever the sacred bond between the Nightshades and the Obsidian Cloud.

Determined to protect this legacy, Orion began formulating a plan. "We need to fortify the monastery. The Shadowed One will come for us again, but this time we will be ready."

Elder Zephyrus agreed, his voice resolute. "We will stand with you, Orion. The bond between the Nightshades and the sky monks is unbreakable. We will defend it with our lives."

The following days were a whirlwind of activity. Orion, with the help of Aria and the monks, trained tirelessly, harnessing the power of the cloud and mastering the air manipulation abilities that were his birthright. Vayla, with her youthful enthusiasm and sharp mind, uncovered more secrets within the monastery, finding hidden chambers and ancient weapons that could aid them in the coming battle.

One evening, as Orion stood on the monastery's highest tower, he felt a deep connection with the cloud. It was as if he could feel its energy flowing through him, strengthening him, preparing him for the inevitable confrontation.

The chapter culminated in a powerful moment where Orion, surrounded by the monks, made a solemn vow. "My ancestors gave their lives to protect this legacy. I will do the same. We will not let the Obsidian Cloud fall into the hands of those who seek to destroy it."

The monks echoed his vow, their voices a united front against the darkness that threatened them. They were ready to face whatever came next, together as one.

As the moon rose high above the monastery, casting its silvery glow on the Obsidian Cloud, Orion Nightshade stood tall, a warrior sage ready to defend his legacy, a legacy that was now revealed in its true, awe-inspiring light.

Chapter 11

Dawn crested over the floating monastery, bathing it in a golden hue, as Orion Nightshade stood with Elder Zephyrus, Aria Windwhisper, and the other sky monks, preparing for the imminent assault. The air was charged with a mixture of tension and determination. This was the day they would defend the legacy of the Obsidian Cloud and the pact that had bound the Nightshade family and the sky monks for centuries.

Orion, now fully aware of his lineage and its significance, felt a surge of power and responsibility coursing through him. He addressed the gathered monks, his voice steady and commanding. "Today, we face a threat that seeks to destroy not just us, but the very essence of the Obsidian Cloud. We stand not only as defenders of this monastery but as protectors of a legacy that transcends time. Together, we will prevail."

Elder Zephyrus, his silver hair glinting in the morning light, nodded approvingly. "We have prepared for this moment. Our faith and our unity will be our greatest weapons. The Obsidian Cloud has always been our protector, and now we shall be its shield."

As they spoke, the sky darkened ominously, a shadow looming on the horizon. The Shadowed One and his aerial assassins approached, a formidable force that seemed to blot out the sun. Orion's eyes narrowed as he sensed the impending battle. "It begins," he declared.

The monastery erupted into action, monks moving into position, their faces etched with resolve. Orion, Aria, and Elder Zephyrus took to the skies, their cloaks billowing around them as they channeled the power of the Obsidian Cloud, manipulating the air to create powerful gusts and barriers.

The aerial assassins descended like a swarm, their movements swift and deadly. But Orion and his allies were prepared. Aria, with her ethereal grace, danced through the sky, her attacks precise and lethal. Orion, his powers amplified by his connection to the cloud, fought with a ferocity that was both awe-inspiring and terrifying.

Below, the sky monks, led by Master Callum and Vayla, utilized ancient artifacts and spells to defend the monastery. Their chants echoed through the air, creating a protective aura around the structure.

The battle raged, a maelstrom of magic, steel, and determination. Orion found himself face to face with The Shadowed One, their duel a clash of shadows and light. Every move Orion made was countered by his enigmatic foe, but he did not falter. He remembered his ancestors, their sacrifices, and the weight of the legacy he carried.

In the midst of the chaos, a turning point occurred. Elder Zephyrus, combining his power with Orion's, unleashed a colossal wave of energy, dispersing a group of assassins and leaving The Shadowed One exposed. Seizing the opportunity, Orion struck with all his might, fueled by the strength of his heritage.

The Shadowed One fell, defeated, his plans unraveled. The remaining assassins, seeing their leader vanquished, retreated into the sky, their threat diminished but not entirely quelled.

As calm returned, the monastery stood, a testament to the resilience and bravery of its defenders. Orion, exhausted yet triumphant, joined his companions. Elder Zephyrus placed a hand on his shoulder, a gesture of respect and gratitude. "You have honored your family and the pact, Orion. Today, you have proven yourself to be the true guardian of the Obsidian Cloud."

Aria smiled warmly at Orion, her eyes reflecting pride and admiration. "Your strength and courage have inspired us all. You have united us in a way that will be remembered for generations."

Orion looked out over the monastery, his heart swelling with a mixture of pride and relief. He had faced his destiny and emerged victorious. But he knew this was not the end. There would be more challenges, more threats to the legacy of the Obsidian Cloud.

As the sun set, casting long shadows across the floating monastery, Orion realized that his journey was far from over. It was merely a chapter in the ongoing saga of the Orion Legacy. But for now, they had won a crucial victory, one that would echo through the annals of time.

The monks gathered, their voices joining in a song of victory and remembrance. Orion stood among them, a beacon of hope and a symbol of the unbreakable bond between the Nightshade family and the sky monks. The Obsidian Cloud swirled above them, a silent witness to the unyielding spirit of those who had sworn to protect it.

This battle was over, but Orion Nightshade's story was just beginning. The legacy of the Obsidian Sky would live on, a legacy of shadows and light, of magic and might, of sacrifice and destiny.

Chapter 12

In the aftermath of the monumental battle, the floating monastery stood silent, a serene testament to the resilience of its defenders and the Obsidian Cloud. The sky, once a battleground, now displayed a tranquil tapestry of colors as dawn broke. Orion Nightshade, standing at the edge of the monastery, gazed into the horizon, his thoughts a whirlwind of reflection and anticipation.

Elder Zephyrus joined him, his presence calm and reassuring. "You have done well, Orion. Your bravery and wisdom have not only saved the monastery but have also honored the pact your family made with us centuries ago."

Orion nodded, his eyes still fixed on the sky. "It feels surreal, Elder Zephyrus. For so long, my family's legacy was a mystery, a source of doubt and confusion. Now, it's as clear as the sky before us. But with clarity comes new questions, new paths to explore."

Aria Windwhisper approached, her face aglow with the light of the rising sun. "The journey never truly ends, Orion. Each step we take leads to new discoveries, new challenges. You've opened a door to a world larger than we imagined."

Vayla, the young novice monk, joined the group, her eyes wide with wonder and respect. "You've shown us all that the past isn't just a story written in books. It lives within us, guiding and shaping our future."

Orion turned to his companions, a smile tugging at the corners of his mouth. "The journey has indeed changed me. I've learned that our legacies are not just about honoring the past but about forging our own paths, making choices that define who we are."

Master Callum, holding ancient texts under his arm, approached the group. "Your journey has also unearthed knowledge long forgotten. The texts you've helped recover will take us years to study. They speak of realms beyond our comprehension, secrets of the Obsidian Cloud that we have yet to understand."

Orion's gaze returned to the sky, contemplative. "Then our journey is far from over. The Obsidian Cloud is more than just a symbol of our pact; it's a key to understanding the mysteries of this world and perhaps others."

Elder Zephyrus placed a hand on Orion's shoulder. "You have a rare gift, Orion. You've united us in purpose and spirit. The path ahead is unknown, but I believe you are the one to lead us forward."

Aria nodded in agreement. "And you won't be alone. We, the sky monks, will stand with you. Together, we will explore these new realms and protect the legacy of the Obsidian Cloud."

Orion looked at each of them, his heart swelling with a sense of camaraderie and purpose. "Then let us embark on this journey together. The Obsidian Sky has many secrets, and I am ready to uncover them."

As the group dispersed to attend to the monastery's repairs and studies, Orion stayed behind, his eyes still fixed on the horizon. The battle had ended, but his journey was just beginning. He knew that the road ahead would be filled with challenges and wonders beyond his imagination.

The monastery, once a place of solitude and mystery, had become a beacon of hope and discovery. Orion realized that his legacy was not just about honoring his ancestors but about creating a legacy of his own, one that would inspire future generations to seek the truth and embrace their destiny.

As the sun rose higher, casting its golden light over the monastery, Orion Nightshade, the guardian of the Obsidian Cloud, the uniter of past and future, stood ready to face whatever lay ahead. His journey had led him to this point, and now a new chapter awaited, filled with adventure, mystery, and the eternal pursuit of knowledge.

The story of Orion's Legacy was far from over. It was, in fact, a new beginning, a journey into the heart of a legacy shrouded in magic and wonder, a journey that would continue to unfold under the vast, ever-changing sky of the Obsidian Cloud.

The Crystal Cavern

Chapter 1

Orion Nightshade's breath formed icy clouds in the frigid Arctic air, each exhale a ghostly whisper against the stark, endless white. Clad in his dark cloak, he trudged through the snow, his boots leaving deep impressions in the untouched blanket of white. His deep, dark eyes, reflecting an inner world as complex as the labyrinthine paths he navigated, scanned the horizon. The Arctic was unforgiving, but Orion, with his lithe, athletic build and cat-like agility, moved with a stealthy grace that belied the harshness of the environment.

His mind was as active as his steps, always calculating, always considering. The rumors of a hidden monastery in these uncharted depths had lured him here, a beacon in his constant search for knowledge and artifacts of power. Orion's journey had always been one of self-discovery, but here in the Arctic, it felt more like a pilgrimage, a test of his resilience and resolve.

As night began to fall, the Arctic sky transformed into a canvas of breathtaking beauty. Orion paused, his sharp, angular features softening in the ethereal glow of the Northern Lights. This natural marvel seemed to echo the magic that he had always felt pulsing in his veins, a reminder of the mysteries he sought to unravel.

Suddenly, his attention snapped to a distant shape emerging from the white landscape. Squinting, Orion discerned a figure moving towards him. His hand instinctively went to the ancient amulet around his neck, feeling its familiar contours. It was a small token of his heritage but a potent reminder of the powers that lay dormant within him.

The figure approached, a cloaked silhouette against the snow. "Orion Nightshade, I presume?" the stranger's voice was deep, resonant.

Orion's gaze narrowed. "Who's asking?"

"I am a friend," the stranger replied, lowering his hood to reveal a weathered face marked by time and wisdom. "I've been expecting you."

Orion studied him cautiously. "You know of me?"

The man nodded. "The monks of the crystal cave monastery sent me. They've sensed your arrival."

A flicker of surprise crossed Orion's features. He had not anticipated such a reception. "Lead the way, then," he said, his voice a blend of curiosity and caution.

They journeyed in silence, the only sound the crunch of snow beneath their feet. As they moved, Orion felt a strange sensation, a pulsing energy that seemed to grow stronger with each step. The monastery was near, he realized, and with it, the artifact that had drawn him into this frozen wasteland.

Finally, the stranger halted, pointing ahead. There, carved into the side of a towering glacier, was the entrance to the monastery. It was a magnificent sight, the architecture ancient and intricate, blending seamlessly with the ice.

"This is it," the stranger said, a hint of reverence in his tone. "The crystal cave monastery."

Orion's eyes widened in awe. He had heard tales of such places, but to see one in person was something else entirely. He stepped forward, feeling the weight of history and mystery enveloping him.

As he crossed the threshold, the air inside the monastery was surprisingly warm. The walls glistened with embedded crystals, casting prismatic light throughout the cavernous space. It was like stepping into another world, a realm where the boundaries between the physical and the psychic blurred.

Orion's guide led him deeper into the monastery, through corridors that echoed with the silent whispers of the past. Finally, they arrived at a large chamber. In its center stood an artifact, its surface pulsating with a strange, rhythmic light.

"This is what you came for, isn't it?" the stranger asked, watching Orion closely.

Orion's gaze was fixed on the artifact. He could feel its energy, a siren call to the depths of his soul. This was more than just a relic; it was a gateway to powers he had yet to comprehend.

"Yes," Orion replied, his voice barely above a whisper. "This is why I'm here."

The stranger nodded solemnly. "Be careful, Orion Nightshade. Some paths, once taken, cannot be undone."

Orion turned to him, a determined glint in his eye. "I've walked many paths," he said. "And I'm ready for whatever this one has in store for me."

With that, Orion reached out towards the artifact, feeling the surge of energy coursing through him. The chapter of his journey in the Arctic had just begun, and the crystal cave monastery was about to reveal its secrets.

As his fingers brushed against the artifact, a wave of psychic energy flooded through him, awakening dormant powers and igniting a fire of discovery in his soul. Orion Nightshade's adventure in the crystal cavern was underway, a journey that would challenge him in ways he never imagined.

Chapter 2

Orion Nightshade's first steps into the crystal cave monastery felt like crossing into a realm where time stood still. The air was heavy with the scent of ancient stone and ice, the walls alive with the shimmer of embedded crystals. His guide, a silent, hooded figure, led him through the labyrinthine corridors, their footsteps echoing softly.

The monastery was a marvel, an architectural wonder carved into the heart of the glacier. The walls glowed faintly, reflecting the light from the crystals in a mesmerizing dance of colors. Orion's eyes, accustomed to darkness, absorbed every detail, every nuance of this hidden sanctuary.

As they dove deeper, the guide finally spoke. "This place is ancient, Orion Nightshade. Older than any recorded history. The monks who built it sought to protect something invaluable."

Orion glanced at him. "The artifact?"

The guide nodded. "Yes, but not just that. It's also about protecting knowledge, the kind that can either enlighten or destroy."

They arrived at a vast chamber, its ceiling arching high above, adorned with intricate carvings. At the center, a group of monks, cloaked in robes of deep blue, stood in a semi-circle. Their presence was serene yet formidable, guardians of the secrets that lay within these walls.

The head monk stepped forward, his eyes meeting Orion's. "Welcome, Orion Nightshade. We have long awaited your arrival."

Orion bowed slightly, a gesture of respect. "I'm honored, but I must know— why me?"

The monk's voice was calm, yet it carried an undeniable authority. "You possess a rare alignment with the psychic energies that permeate this place. Your coming was foretold in our prophecies."

Orion's mind raced. Prophecies? His arrival foretold? The pieces of the puzzle were beginning to form a picture, but it was one that raised more questions than answers.

"What exactly do you expect from me?" Orion asked, his tone laced with a mix of curiosity and skepticism.

The monk gestured towards a secluded alcove. "We wish to show you the true purpose of this monastery and the role you are destined to play."

As Orion followed, he noticed the intricate patterns on the walls, each telling a story of cosmic battles, of balance between light and dark. The alcove housed a pedestal on which lay an ancient tome, its pages yellowed with age.

"This is the Chronicle of the Crystal Cavern," the monk explained. "It contains the history of our order and the prophecies of the psychic realm."

Orion ran his fingers over the tome's cover, feeling a surge of energy. The tome seemed to pulsate with a life of its own.

"The artifact you seek," the monk continued, "is deeply connected to these prophecies. It is a key that unlocks psychic potentials, but in untrained hands, it could bring catastrophe."

Orion looked up sharply. "Catastrophe?"

The monk nodded gravely. "There are forces that seek to exploit this power. The Mind Syndicate, a shadowy group with dangerous intentions."

Orion felt a chill run down his spine. The Mind Syndicate. He had heard rumors, whispers of a group that dove into the darkest aspects of psychic manipulation. Was this why he was drawn here?

"You must understand the artifact and its power to stand against them," the monk said. "We will guide you, teach you what we know. But the journey is yours alone."

Orion felt the weight of the responsibility settling on his shoulders. This was more than a mere adventure; it was a call to a destiny he hadn't foreseen.

"I'll need to understand more about this artifact and the syndicate," Orion said, his voice firm. "I'm no stranger to danger, but I won't walk blindly into a battle I don't understand."

The monks exchanged glances, a silent communication passing between them. Finally, the head monk nodded. "Very well. Follow me."

They led Orion to a hidden chamber, its walls lined with ancient texts and artifacts. In the center, under a beam of light that seemed to emanate from the crystals themselves, was the artifact—a crystalline structure, glowing with an inner light that pulsed rhythmically.

Orion approached it cautiously, feeling a resonance within him, a connection that seemed to bridge the gap between his own psychic energy and that of the artifact.

"This is the Heart of the Cavern," the monk said. "It is an amplifier of psychic energy, a conduit between the physical and the psychic realms."

Orion reached out, hesitating for a moment before touching the crystal. A flood of visions and sensations overwhelmed him, images of past, present, and possible futures swirling in a kaleidoscope of psychic energy.

He staggered back, gasping for breath. The monks watched, their expressions a mix of concern and expectation.

"You have begun your journey,

Orion Nightshade," the head monk said. "The path ahead is fraught with peril, but also with the potential for great enlightenment."

Orion steadied himself, his mind racing with the possibilities and dangers that lay ahead. The hidden monastery had revealed its secret, and with it, his role in a much larger tapestry of cosmic struggle.

As he left the chamber, Orion knew that his adventure had taken a turn into uncharted realms, realms where the boundaries of reality were as fluid and elusive as the Northern Lights that danced above the Arctic ice. The journey into the heart of the crystal cavern had just begun, and Orion Nightshade was at its epicenter, a reluctant hero in a battle that spanned the psychic realms.

Chapter 3

In the heart of the crystal cave monastery, Orion Nightshade stood before the pulsating artifact, the Heart of the Cavern. Its luminescence bathed the chamber in a spectral light, casting elongated shadows that danced along the walls. The monks, solemn and watchful, encircled him, their eyes reflecting the artifact's glow.

Orion reached out tentatively, his fingers hovering above the crystal's surface. A surge of energy, raw and unbridled, coursed through him, awakening a dormant power within. His head reeled as visions flashed before his eyes - fragments of unknown memories, whispers of forgotten lore. The monks watched in silence, their expressions a blend of anticipation and concern.

The head monk, a figure of serene authority, stepped forward. "The artifact resonates with your psychic essence, Orion. It is awakening abilities within you, abilities that are both a gift and a burden."

Orion withdrew his hand, steadying himself against the overwhelming tide of energy. "What kind of abilities?" he asked, his voice a mix of wonder and unease.

"You possess the power to tap into the psychic realm, to see beyond the veil of the physical world," the monk explained. "But such power comes with great responsibility. It must be wielded with wisdom and restraint."

Orion nodded, the weight of the monk's words settling upon him. He was no stranger to power, but this was different, deeper, more intrinsic to his very being.

The monks led Orion to a secluded part of the monastery, a chamber filled with ancient scrolls and artifacts. "To master your abilities, you must first understand them," the head monk said, gesturing towards the scrolls.

Orion spent hours poring over the ancient texts, absorbing their knowledge. The scrolls spoke of the psychic realm, a dimension beyond the physical, where thoughts and emotions held sway. He learned of those who had walked this path before, their triumphs and their tragedies.

As the days passed, Orion began to experience the world in a way he never had before. He could sense the emotions of those around him, hear the unspoken thoughts that lingered in their minds. It was a revelation and a challenge, for with this newfound sensitivity came a vulnerability to the overwhelming cacophony of the human psyche.

One evening, as Orion meditated in the chamber, he felt a presence, a whisper in the back of his mind. He opened his eyes to find the head monk watching him, a knowing look in his eyes.

"You are progressing well, Orion. But there is more to learn," the monk said. "The artifact is not just a source of power; it is a gateway, a bridge to the psychic realm. You must learn to traverse this realm, to navigate its perils and harness its potential."

Orion felt a thrill of excitement mixed with apprehension. The psychic realm was a frontier of infinite possibilities, a domain where the constraints of the physical world no longer applied.

Under the monks' guidance, Orion began to explore this new realm. He learned to extend his consciousness beyond his physical body, to journey through the landscape of the mind. It was a surreal experience, traveling through a world shaped by thoughts and emotions, where reality was fluid and ever-changing.

But with each journey, Orion felt a growing sense of unease. He sensed a darkness lurking in the psychic realm, a malevolent force that watched him with interest. The monks warned him of the dangers, of entities that dwelled in the deeper reaches of the mind.

"The psychic realm is a reflection of the collective consciousness of humanity," the head monk explained. "It contains both light and dark, hope and despair. You must be vigilant, for there are those who would use this realm for their own ends."

Orion realized that the threat of the Mind Syndicate was not just a physical one. They were players in this psychic domain, masters of manipulation who sought to bend the will of others to their desires.

Armed with this knowledge, Orion knew that he must confront the syndicate, not just in the physical world but in the psychic realm as well. It was a battle on two fronts, a struggle for the very soul of humanity.

As he prepared for this confrontation, Orion felt a change within himself. He was no longer just an adventurer, a seeker of artifacts. He was a guardian, a protector of the psychic realm and all who dwelled within it. The journey through the crystal cave monastery had transformed him, forging him into a warrior of the mind.

And so, with the monks' blessing, Orion Nightshade set out from the monastery, his resolve strengthened, his purpose clear. The battle against the Mind Syndicate awaited, and he was ready to face it head-on, armed with the powers of the psychic realm and the wisdom of the ancient monks.

The adventure was far from over, and Orion knew that the path ahead would be fraught with danger. But he was no longer the man who had entered the monastery. He was something more, something greater - a beacon of light in a world shrouded in shadows.

Chapter 4

The chill of the Arctic night was a stark contrast to the warmth of the crystal cave monastery. Orion Nightshade, now attuned to the psychic energies of the artifact, felt a sense of urgency. The knowledge of the Mind Syndicate and their nefarious intentions weighed heavily on him. It was time to confront this new threat.

Orion, cloaked in darkness, moved stealthily through the icy landscape. His senses, heightened by his newfound abilities, alerted him to the presence of others long before he saw them. Hidden in the shadows, he observed a group of figures gathered around a campfire. They were members of the Mind Syndicate, the very threat the monks had warned him about.

The leader of the group, a charismatic figure with a commanding presence, was speaking passionately. Orion edged closer, using his psychic abilities to eavesdrop on their conversation.

"We must find the monastery and claim the artifact," the leader declared. "It is the key to our vision. With it, we can reshape the world."

Orion's grip tightened on the ancient amulet around his neck, a silent vow to protect the monastery and its secrets. He knew he had to act.

Using the cover of night, Orion infiltrated their camp. He was a shadow among shadows, his movements silent and precise. He overheard plans, names, locations - valuable information that would help him thwart their scheme.

Suddenly, a syndicate member, more perceptive than the rest, sensed Orion's presence. "Who's there?" he called out, scanning the darkness.

Orion acted quickly, using his psychic abilities to cloud the man's mind, casting an illusion of emptiness where he hid. The man shook his head, dismissing his suspicion, and Orion seized the opportunity to retreat into the night.

Back at the monastery, Orion shared his findings with the monks. "They're planning to raid the monastery. They know about the artifact and its power."

The head monk nodded gravely. "We have feared this day would come. The Mind Syndicate does not understand the true nature of the artifact. In their hands, it could bring about a catastrophe."

Orion's resolve hardened. "Then we must prepare. We cannot let them succeed."

Over the next few days, the monastery became a fortress. Orion, with his unique blend of agility and stealth, trained with the monks, honing his psychic abilities for the confrontation ahead.

One evening, as Orion meditated in the chamber of the Heart of the Cavern, he felt a ripple in the psychic realm. The syndicate was on the move, their intentions a dark wave crashing against the shores of his mind.

The attack came at dawn. The syndicate, armed and ruthless, breached the monastery's defenses. Orion was ready. He met them with a ferocity that surprised even himself. His body moved with the grace of a predator, while his mind weaved psychic illusions, disorienting his attackers.

The battle was intense, a maelstrom of physical prowess and psychic power. Orion fought alongside the monks, their combined strength holding the syndicate at bay.

The leader of the syndicate, seeing his forces faltering, confronted Orion. "You don't understand what's at stake," he hissed. "We are trying to save the world."

Orion parried his attacks, countering with his own. "Your vision is flawed. Power without wisdom is a path to destruction."

The leader, frustrated and enraged, unleashed a powerful psychic blast. Orion, drawing on the energy of the artifact, absorbed the attack, redirecting it back at the syndicate leader.

Defeated and disoriented, the leader retreated, his forces following suit. The monastery was safe, for now.

In the aftermath, the monks praised Orion's bravery. "You have protected not just the monastery but the balance of the psychic realm," the head monk said.

Orion looked at the Heart of the Cavern, its glow a soft reassurance. "The syndicate will return. And I must be ready."

The head monk placed a hand on Orion's shoulder. "You have proven yourself a true guardian. We will aid you in your preparation. The battle may be over, but the war is just beginning."

Orion nodded, a sense of purpose fueling his determination. He had faced the Mind Syndicate and emerged victorious. But he knew this was just the beginning of a larger conflict, one that would test the limits of his abilities and the strength of his resolve.

As he gazed at the stars above the Arctic horizon, Orion Nightshade understood that his journey had taken a new turn. No longer was he a mere adventurer; he was a guardian of the psychic realm, a warrior against the forces that sought to misuse its power. The path ahead was fraught with danger, but he was ready to face whatever came his way. The legacy of the crystal cave monastery was in his hands, and he would protect it at all costs.

Chapter 5

The aftermath of the skirmish with the Mind Syndicate left a profound impact on Orion Nightshade. Inside the crystal cave monastery, he found himself wrestling with the burgeoning powers that now coursed through him, a storm of psychic energy that threatened to overwhelm his senses.

As he sat in the monastery's meditation chamber, the monks gathered around him, their expressions etched with concern. The head monk, a wise figure who had become a mentor to Orion, spoke gently, "You have tapped into powers that many cannot fathom, Orion. It is a path fraught with peril, and you must tread carefully."

Orion's eyes, usually so deep and contemplative, now flickered with a turmoil that mirrored his internal struggle. "I feel these powers consuming me," he admitted. "Every moment is a battle to maintain control."

The monks nodded in understanding. "This is the trial of the mind," one of them explained. "You must learn to master your abilities, to bend them to your will rather than be ruled by them."

Over the following days, Orion underwent rigorous training. He learned ancient techniques to harness his psychic energy, to channel it in ways that would not only aid him in battle but also in understanding the deeper mysteries of the mind.

One exercise involved Orion projecting his consciousness into a realm of mental constructs. Here, he faced his fears, his doubts, and his past – all taking physical forms. He battled these manifestations, each victory bringing him closer to inner peace and control.

However, the greatest challenge came unexpectedly one night. While meditating, Orion's mind was suddenly assaulted by a powerful psychic force. He found himself in a dark, twisted version of the monastery, a realm created by the Mind Syndicate to trap and torment him.

Orion navigated this mindscape, confronting illusions and deceptive memories. He encountered figures from his past, including Zara Cortez, the leader of the Serpent's Fang, who taunted him with his failures and insecurities.

Amidst this chaos, Orion heard a voice, calm and familiar – the head monk. "Remember your training, Orion. Find your center. Your power lies in your will."

Gathering his resolve, Orion fought through the psychic barrage. He focused on his connection to the artifact, drawing on its energy to dispel the illusions. With each step, the false monastery crumbled, revealing the true path of his mind.

Finally, Orion emerged victorious, his psyche intact. He awoke in the real monastery, the monks by his side. "You have passed a crucial test," the head monk said with a hint of pride. "Your mind is your greatest weapon and your staunchest shield."

Orion's journey into his psyche had been harrowing, but it had also been enlightening. He understood now that his powers were not just tools for combat; they were extensions of his being, a means to explore the depths of his soul and the mysteries of the universe.

In the days that followed, Orion's training intensified. He learned to extend his psychic senses, to feel the ebb and flow of energies around him, to communicate thoughts and to shield his mind from intruders. He practiced moving objects with his mind, bending light to become invisible, and even glimpsing fragments of potential futures.

As his mastery grew, so did his understanding of the responsibility that came with such power. He knew that the Mind Syndicate sought to use these abilities for domination, to control minds and bend them to their will. Orion vowed to use his powers to protect, to defend against those who would misuse them.

One evening, as Orion sat gazing at the Arctic sky, the head monk joined him. "You have grown much, Orion," he said. "But remember, the journey of self-discovery is never-ending. Each day brings new challenges and revelations."

Orion nodded, a sense of calm acceptance in his eyes. "I am ready for whatever lies ahead. My trials have strengthened me, in mind and spirit."

The chapter of Orion's trials of the mind had ended, but his journey was far from over. He stood now at the precipice of a greater conflict, armed with powers that transcended the physical realm. The Mind Syndicate remained a looming threat, and Orion knew that the ultimate confrontation was inevitable.

But he was no longer the man who had entered the monastery. He was a warrior of the mind, a guardian of the psychic realm, ready to face the darkness with the light of his newfound abilities. Orion Nightshade's legacy was just beginning to unfold, and the world would soon witness the true extent of his powers.

Chapter 6

In the serene stillness of the crystal cave monastery, Orion Nightshade reflected on his recent trials and the looming threat of the Mind Syndicate. His thoughts were interrupted by the arrival of a group of monks, their faces etched with urgency. The head monk, a figure of calm wisdom, stepped forward.

"Orion, time is of the essence," he began. "We have sensed a shift in the psychic realm. The syndicate's actions are accelerating, and we fear they may be close to locating the monastery."

Orion's eyes narrowed, a flash of determination lighting them up. "Then we must act. But I am one, and they are many. I need allies."

The head monk nodded in agreement. "Indeed. And allies you shall have. We have contacted a group that can aid you. They are not of our monastery, but they share our goal of protecting the psychic realm."

A sense of intrigue and a flicker of hope stirred within Orion. "Who are they?"

"They are a collective of individuals, each with unique abilities and insights into the psychic realm. They have been fighting the syndicate in their own ways," the monk explained.

Later that day, in a secluded chamber of the monastery, Orion met with this newfound alliance. The group was diverse, each member possessing skills that complemented the others. There was a woman who could read auras and emotions, a man with the ability to project his thoughts into others' minds, and another who could see brief glimpses of the future.

Orion listened intently as they shared their experiences and knowledge of the syndicate. The woman, whose name was Aria, spoke of how the syndicate had tried to manipulate her ability for their own ends. The mind projector, named Darius, recounted his narrow escape from the syndicate's clutches. The seer, known as Eldon, spoke in riddles, his visions providing cryptic warnings of possible futures.

As the group strategized, Orion felt a kinship with these strangers. They were united by a common purpose - to thwart the syndicate's plans and protect the psychic realm. Orion shared his own experiences and the knowledge he had gained from the monks and the artifact.

A plan began to take shape. They would use their combined abilities to locate the syndicate's stronghold and disrupt their operations. Orion would be the spearhead of the operation, given his training and connection to the monastery's artifact.

The alliance spent days in preparation, honing their abilities and forming a cohesive unit. Orion found himself growing particularly close to Aria, her empathic abilities providing him with a deeper understanding of his own emotions and the turmoil he had been facing.

One night, as Orion and Aria sat under the starlit sky, she turned to him. "You carry a heavy burden, Orion. But remember, you're not alone in this fight. We're with you."

Orion looked at her, the moonlight reflecting in his dark eyes. "I've always walked my path alone. It's... unfamiliar, having allies."

Aria smiled gently. "Sometimes, the most unexpected paths lead us to where we need to be."

The day of the operation arrived. The group, led by Orion, set out under the cover of darkness. They journeyed through the Arctic wilderness, their destination a remote area where Eldon's visions had indicated the presence of the syndicate.

As they neared the location, Darius projected a psychic shield to mask their approach, while Aria provided emotional insights, warning them of any impending danger.

Finally, they reached the syndicate's hidden facility, a fortress of sorts, nestled in a secluded valley. The group infiltrated the compound, their diverse abilities complementing each other, creating openings where there seemed to be none.

Inside, they encountered members of the syndicate. Battles ensued, a chaotic blend of psychic and physical confrontations. Orion was at the forefront, his training with the monks making him a formidable adversary. He moved with purpose and precision, his mind focused and clear.

The group fought their way to the heart of the compound, where they discovered the syndicate's plan - a device that could amplify psychic energy to a catastrophic scale. The syndicate intended to use it to bend the will of nations.

Working together, the alliance disrupted the device, halting the syndicate's plan. In the midst of the conflict, the leader of the syndicate appeared, confronting Orion. Their battle was intense, a clash of wills and powers.

Orion, drawing on the strength of his allies and the training he had received, overpowered the syndicate leader. The facility was secured, the immediate threat neutralized.

As they returned to the monastery, Orion felt a sense of accomplishment, but also a realization that the war was far from over. The syndicate was still out there, its reach far and wide.

The head monk greeted them upon their return. "You have done well, Orion, and your allies have proven their worth. This is a significant victory, but the path ahead remains perilous."

Orion nodded, his resolve unwavering. "We will be ready. Together, we are stronger."

That night, as Orion gazed at the stars, he reflected on the bonds he had formed with his unlikely allies. The journey had taught him the value of trust and collaboration. He was no longer a lone warrior in the shadows; he was part of a collective, a force united against a common enemy.

Chapter 7

In the relative calm following their victory over the syndicate's facility, Orion Nightshade and his new allies gathered in the monastery's grand hall. The atmosphere was tense, the weight of unanswered questions hanging heavily in the air.

Orion, his features more contemplative than ever, broke the silence. "We've halted their immediate plans, but we know little of their ultimate goal. We need to understand what drives the Mind Syndicate, what their endgame is."

Aria, the empath, shared her insights. "There's more to their actions than mere lust for power. I sensed confusion and fear among them, not the certainty of fanatics."

Darius, the mind projector, nodded in agreement. "Their leader, he's driven by something more complex. There's a desperation in his actions."

Eldon, the seer, spoke up, his voice tinged with unease. "My visions are clouded, but one thing is clear – the syndicate is racing against time. They're afraid, not just ambitious."

The group turned their attention to a set of documents recovered from the syndicate's compound, hoping to find clues. As Orion sifted through the papers, a particular document caught his eye. It was a series of correspondence between the syndicate's leader and an unknown figure.

As he read aloud, the pieces of the puzzle began to fall into place. The syndicate believed that a psychic catastrophe was imminent, a disaster that would unravel the fabric of the psychic realm and spill over into the physical world. Their goal was not world domination but prevention of this catastrophe.

The revelation hit Orion like a wave. "They think they're saving the world," he murmured, a mix of disbelief and realization in his voice.

Aria looked thoughtful. "If they're right, then we're not just against them. We're against a ticking clock."

The head monk, who had been listening intently, spoke softly, "The psychic realm is delicate, connected intimately to the physical world. If they're correct, this catastrophe could be disastrous for both realms."

Orion stood up, determination etched on his face. "We need to verify their claims. If there's truth to this, we must reassess our approach."

The group agreed to a plan. Orion and his allies would seek out sources that could validate the syndicate's fears. This journey took them beyond the monastery, into the forgotten corners of the psychic realm and the hidden archives of ancient knowledge.

Their quest led them to remote locations – libraries buried under deserts, sanctuaries hidden in mountain ranges, and realms within the psychic world that were both wondrous and terrifying. Throughout their journey, Orion's abilities grew, as did his understanding of the intricate tapestry of the psychic realm.

In a hidden library in the Himalayas, they found ancient prophecies speaking of a 'Rift', a tear in the fabric of the psychic realm that could lead to chaos in both worlds. In a sanctuary in the Andes, they encountered a group of psychic scholars who spoke of the 'Harmonic Convergence', a rare cosmic event that could either heal or shatter the psychic realm.

Armed with this knowledge, Orion and his allies returned to the monastery. The head monk listened gravely to their findings. "It appears the syndicate may have been acting out of a misguided attempt to prevent a greater evil," he said solemnly.

Orion pondered their next move. "If the syndicate is acting out of fear for this catastrophe, perhaps we can reason with them, work together to find a solution."

Aria agreed. "Understanding is the key. We need to communicate, not just confront."

The chapter closed with Orion and his allies preparing to reach out to the syndicate, to open a dialogue in the hopes of finding a common ground. The realization that their enemy might have been driven by a shared fear of a greater threat changed the nature of their conflict.

Orion, once a solitary figure in the shadows, now stood at the center of a complex web of alliances and conflicts, his role not just that of a warrior but also a mediator. The path ahead was uncertain, but he was ready to walk it, guided by his newfound wisdom and the support of his allies. The journey through the crystal cave monastery had transformed him, and he would use this transformation to navigate the treacherous waters of the conflict that lay ahead.

Chapter 8

Back at the crystal cave monastery, Orion Nightshade, now aware of the syndicate's true intentions, found himself at a crossroads. With his allies around him in the monastery's grand hall, he pondered their next move.

"The syndicate seeks to prevent a psychic catastrophe," Orion mused. "We share a common goal, yet our methods differ greatly. We must find a way to avert this disaster without resorting to their extreme measures."

Aria spoke up, her voice steady, "To do that, we need a deeper understanding of the psychic realm and the forces at play. Your mastery of the mind is key, Orion."

Orion nodded in agreement. "The monastery's artifact and the teachings of the monks have opened new paths to me. I must dive deeper, push the boundaries of what I've learned."

The head monk, always a guiding presence, suggested a course of action. "The monastery holds ancient texts that speak of the Harmonic Convergence, a rare alignment of psychic energies. Understanding this phenomenon could be crucial."

Orion spent the following days immersed in study and meditation, absorbing the monastery's vast knowledge. He learned to extend his psychic perception, to sense the subtle flows of energy that connected all things. His training took him to the very edge of the psychic realm, where he glimpsed the intricate web of psychic forces that bound the universe.

With each passing day, his mastery grew. His mind, once a battleground of conflicting energies, now became a well of calm and focus. He honed his abilities to project his thoughts, to shield his mind from intrusion, and to tap into the psychic echoes of the past.

One night, as Orion meditated in the chamber of the Heart of the Cavern, he experienced a breakthrough. His consciousness expanded, transcending the physical boundaries of the monastery. He found himself in a vast, ethereal landscape, where the psychic energies of the world converged.

In this realm, Orion encountered a presence, an ancient consciousness that had dwelled in the psychic realm for eons. It spoke to him in a language beyond words, imparting wisdom about the Harmonic Convergence and the nature of the impending catastrophe.

Orion learned that the Harmonic Convergence was more than just an alignment of energies; it was a gateway, a point of connection between the physical and psychic realms. The impending catastrophe was a result of this gateway becoming unstable, threatening to tear the fabric of both worlds.

Armed with this knowledge, Orion returned to his physical body, a sense of urgency fueling his actions. He shared his revelations with his allies, explaining the critical nature of their task.

"We must stabilize the Convergence," Orion declared. "If we can harmonize the psychic energies, we can avert the catastrophe."

The group set to work, formulating a plan to harness the monastery's artifact and Orion's abilities to stabilize the Convergence. As the days passed, Orion's connection to the psychic realm deepened, his abilities reaching heights he never thought possible.

The moment of the Convergence drew near. Orion and his allies prepared for a ritual that would require all their strength and focus. The monastery became a focal point of psychic energy, the artifact at its heart pulsating with power.

As the ritual commenced, Orion took his place at the center, his mind a conduit for the immense energies they sought to control. His allies, each in their positions, lent their strength to the effort, their combined wills bending the psychic forces to their purpose.

The ritual was intense, a maelstrom of psychic power that tested the limits of Orion's abilities. He felt the energies of the Convergence flow through him, a torrent that threatened to overwhelm his senses.

But Orion held firm, his mastery of the mind guiding him through the storm. He channeled the energies, weaving them into a harmonious pattern that resonated with the artifact's core.

As the ritual reached its climax, a brilliant light enveloped the monastery, the psychic energies harmonizing in a perfect balance. The threat of the catastrophe was averted, the gateway stabilized.

Exhausted but triumphant, Orion and his allies celebrated their victory. They had not only prevented a disaster but had also achieved a deeper understanding of the psychic realm and their place within it.

Orion, once a lone guardian of ancient secrets, had evolved into a master of the mind, a bridge between worlds. His journey had taken him to the depths of his own psyche and the far reaches of the universe, forging him into a figure of immense power and wisdom.

Chapter 9

In the aftermath of the Harmonic Convergence, the monastery was a place of both triumph and deep contemplation. Orion Nightshade, now recognized as a Master of the Mind, gathered with his allies in the ancient hall, their faces illuminated by the flickering candlelight.

Orion, his eyes reflecting a maturity beyond his years, addressed the group. "We've averted one disaster, but our journey is far from over. The syndicate's fear of a psychic catastrophe was not unfounded. We must prepare for what lies ahead."

The head monk, an ever-present figure of wisdom, nodded gravely. "The Harmonic Convergence has stabilized the psychic realm for now, but it is a delicate balance. The catastrophe that looms is a threat not just to us, but to the very fabric of reality."

Orion turned to Aria, whose empathic abilities had grown stronger. "What do your senses tell you, Aria?"

She closed her eyes, reaching out with her mind. "There's a disturbance, like a ripple across a still pond. It's subtle but growing stronger."

Eldon, the seer, spoke next, his voice tinged with urgency. "My visions are becoming clearer. There's a darkness at the edge of the psychic realm, a force that seeks to consume and corrupt."

Darius added, "We need to understand this darkness. If we're to fight it, we must know its nature."

Orion, resolute in his duty, made a decision. "We'll split into two groups. Aria, Eldon, and I will venture into the psychic realm to confront this darkness.

Darius, you and the others will stay here with the monks. Guard the monastery and maintain the balance we've achieved."

The following day, Orion, Aria, and Eldon prepared for their journey into the depths of the psychic realm. They entered a deep state of meditation, guided by the monks' chants, their consciousnesses drifting into the vast expanse of the psychic world.

They found themselves in a landscape of surreal beauty, a realm where thoughts and emotions took physical form. As they ventured deeper, the scenery grew darker, the air thick with a sense of foreboding.

Suddenly, they were confronted by a manifestation of the darkness – a swirling mass of shadows and malevolent energy. Orion stepped forward, his mind a bastion against the encroaching gloom.

Aria, sensing the emotions within the darkness, whispered, "There's pain here, and fear. This isn't just a force of destruction; it's something that has been wounded, corrupted."

Eldon, his eyes reflecting the chaos around them, said, "It's a fracture in the psychic realm, a wound that's festering. If left unchecked, it will spread."

Orion, drawing upon the full extent of his abilities, reached out to the darkness. He felt its pain, its anger, but also a flicker of something else – a desire for peace, for healing.

"Listen to me," Orion projected his thoughts into the heart of the darkness. "You are part of the psychic realm, as we all are. Your pain can be healed, but you must let us help you."

The darkness churned, its form shifting, as if struggling with internal conflict. Slowly, the malevolent energy began to recede, revealing a core of pure, untainted psychic power.

Orion, Aria, and Eldon worked together, weaving their abilities to mend the fracture. The task was arduous, demanding every ounce of their strength and concentration.

Back at the monastery, Darius and the remaining allies felt a surge in the psychic realm. They redoubled their efforts, chanting and focusing their energies to support their friends in the psychic world.

After what seemed like an eternity, the fracture was healed, the darkness replaced by a gentle, radiant light. The psychic realm, once threatened by catastrophe, was now whole again.

Orion, Aria, and Eldon returned to their physical bodies, exhausted but victorious. The monastery's hall erupted in cheers and relief as they recounted their journey.

The head monk approached Orion, a look of profound respect in his eyes. "You have done what many thought impossible, Orion. You've healed the psychic realm and averted a catastrophe that could have unraveled reality itself."

Orion, his demeanor humble, replied, "It was a collective effort. Without the strength and unity of all of us, this would not have been possible."

That night, as Orion looked up at the starry sky, he realized that his journey had changed him in ways he could never have imagined. He was no longer just a guardian of ancient secrets; he had become a healer of realms, a bridge between worlds.

Chapter 10

The crystal cave monastery, once a place of serene contemplation, transformed into a battleground of the mind. Orion Nightshade, standing at the precipice of a monumental confrontation, gathered his allies in the dimly lit hall.

"The time has come," Orion declared, his voice echoing off the ancient stone walls. "The leader of the Mind Syndicate is aware of our victory over the psychic catastrophe. He won't stop until he has harnessed the power of the psychic realm for his own purposes."

Eldon, the seer, interjected, "My visions have shown me the syndicate leader's intentions. He believes that controlling the psychic realm is the only way to prevent future catastrophes. His conviction is strong, but his methods are dangerous."

Orion nodded solemnly. "We must confront him, not only to prevent his misuse of psychic powers but to show him there's another way to protect our world."

The group, united by their resolve, prepared for the confrontation. They knew the battle would not be one of swords and shields, but of minds and wills. The monastery became a fortress, its protective energies amplified by the monks.

As night fell, a palpable tension filled the air. The leader of the Mind Syndicate, a charismatic yet imposing figure, arrived at the monastery's entrance, flanked by his most powerful followers. Orion stepped forward to meet him, his allies close behind.

The syndicate leader, his voice laced with power, addressed Orion. "You've meddled in affairs beyond your understanding, Nightshade. The psychic realm must be controlled, or it will bring ruin to us all."

Orion, his stance unwavering, replied, "Control is not the answer. I've seen the potential of the psychic realm, a potential for harmony and understanding. Your path leads only to oppression and fear."

As the two engaged in a verbal sparring, the air crackled with psychic energy. The confrontation escalated as each tried to impose their will upon the other, their mental energies clashing like thunder.

Orion, drawing upon the depths of his newfound mastery, projected a vision into the mind of the syndicate leader. He showed him a world where the psychic realm was respected, where its powers were used for enlightenment and protection, not control.

The syndicate leader, taken aback by the intensity of the vision, faltered momentarily. But his conviction was deep-rooted, and he retaliated with a mental onslaught, trying to dominate Orion's mind with visions of chaos and destruction, the consequences of leaving the psychic realm unchecked.

The battle was fierce, a tempest of psychic energy that threatened to overwhelm both combatants. Orion's allies joined the fray, lending their strengths to bolster Orion's defenses. Aria's empathic abilities countered the syndicate leader's emotional manipulations, while Eldon's visions provided foresight into his next moves.

The monastery itself became an arena of mental might, its ancient walls resonating with the echoes of psychic powers. The monks, chanting in unison, created a barrier of protection, their voices a steady anchor in the storm.

As the battle reached its zenith, Orion, tapping into the very essence of the psychic realm, found a connection to the syndicate leader's mind. He saw the fear and pain that drove him, the burden of responsibility he felt to protect the world in the only way he knew how.

Orion, with a deep sense of empathy, spoke directly to the leader's soul. "I understand your fear, but there's another path, one of balance and unity. Let us guide you towards it."

The syndicate leader, confronted with the sincerity and depth of Orion's conviction, experienced a moment of clarity. His mental barriers crumbled, not under force, but under the realization that his path was not the only one.

The psychic storm subsided, leaving a profound silence in its wake. The syndicate leader, now free from the shackles of his own conviction, looked at Orion with new eyes.

"You have shown me a different way, Nightshade. Perhaps there is hope for coexistence between our worlds," he conceded, his voice devoid of its earlier hostility.

The confrontation ended not with a victor and a vanquished, but with an understanding, a mutual recognition of the complexities and potentials of the psychic realm.

Orion and his allies, weary but heartened, knew that this was a significant step towards a greater harmony between the physical and psychic worlds. They had not only thwarted a threat but had also opened a door to new possibilities, new alliances.

Chapter 11

The aftermath of the psychic battle left a tangible stillness in the air of the crystal cave monastery. Orion Nightshade, his allies by his side, understood that the confrontation with the syndicate's leader was just the beginning. The psychic catastrophe they had narrowly averted was a symptom of a larger imbalance within the psychic realm.

Gathering in the monastery's central chamber, where the ancient artifact resonated with a soothing hum, Orion addressed the group. "We've managed to bring the syndicate leader to our side, but our task isn't over. The psychic realm is still in turmoil. We must stabilize it, or the catastrophe we just avoided will resurface, perhaps in an even more destructive form."

Eldon, the seer, stepped forward, his eyes reflecting the depth of his visions. "The artifact in this monastery is key. It's not just a source of power; it's a conduit that connects deeply with the psychic realm. We must use it to restore balance."

Aria, the empath, added, "The syndicate's actions, though misguided, were a response to the realm's instability. We need to heal the realm, not just for our world but for the countless beings that exist within it."

Orion nodded, feeling the weight of their responsibility. "We'll need to work together, combining our strengths. The artifact will guide us, but it's our unity that will make this possible."

The group formed a circle around the artifact, each member focusing their energy and thoughts on the task at hand. Orion, channeling his newly mastered psychic abilities, initiated the connection with the artifact. A brilliant light emanated from it, enveloping the group in a warm, pulsating glow.

As they dove deeper into the psychic realm, they encountered the rifts and instabilities caused by the syndicate's previous attempts to control it. The realm was a tapestry of thoughts, emotions, and memories, vibrant yet fragile.

Working in unison, they began to mend the rifts. Aria's empathy soothed the realm's agitated emotions, while Eldon's foresight allowed them to anticipate and counteract the cascading effects of the instabilities. Orion, acting as the conduit, directed their collective efforts with precision and care.

The task was arduous, demanding everything they had. The psychic realm responded to their efforts, its energies gradually harmonizing. The once chaotic and disjointed whispers within the realm began to weave into a symphony of balance and peace.

Meanwhile, the syndicate leader, observing their efforts, experienced a profound change. Witnessing the power of unity and understanding, he realized the error of his ways. He approached Orion, offering his assistance. "I was wrong, Nightshade. Your way has shown me that there is more to the psychic realm than control. Let me help."

Orion, acknowledging his genuine change of heart, accepted his offer. Together, they worked, further stabilizing the realm. The leader's knowledge of the psychic energies, combined with the group's efforts, accelerated the healing process.

After hours that felt like an eternity, the realm calmed. The artifact's light dimmed to a gentle glow, signaling the restoration of balance. The group, exhausted but triumphant, shared a moment of quiet celebration.

"We've done it," Orion breathed, relief evident in his voice. "The psychic realm is stable. But we must remain vigilant. Our actions today have shown that balance is a continuous effort."

The monks, having witnessed the extraordinary events, approached Orion. "You have our eternal gratitude, Nightshade. You and your allies have not only saved our monastery but also the psychic realm. This place will always be a sanctuary for you and those who seek understanding of the psychic powers."

As the group prepared to leave the monastery, Orion looked back at the artifact, now silent and serene. He knew this adventure was a significant chapter in his journey, one that had changed him in ways he was still comprehending.

With a newfound sense of purpose and a deeper understanding of his role as a guardian of the psychic realm, Orion Nightshade stepped out of the monastery, ready to face whatever challenges lay ahead. The journey of Orion's Legacy continued, the crystal cavern standing as a testament to their unity and resilience in the face of impending disaster.

Chapter 12

As the arctic sun dipped below the horizon, casting a serene glow over the snow-laden landscape, Orion Nightshade stood at the edge of the monastery's entrance, his eyes reflecting the journey he had undergone. The once hidden monastery, now a symbol of his growth, emanated a peaceful energy, contrasting the turbulent events that had unfolded.

Elena, standing beside him, broke the silence. "You've changed, Orion. The man who entered this monastery isn't the same one standing with me now."

Orion nodded, his gaze still fixed on the horizon. "I've learned that power is not just about control. It's about understanding, balance, and the connections we share with everything around us."

The monks, emerging from the monastery, approached Orion with reverence. The eldest among them, a wise sage with eyes as deep as the ocean, spoke, "You have not only saved our sanctuary but also taught us invaluable lessons. Your journey here will be remembered and passed down through generations."

Orion humbly acknowledged their words. "I am but a traveler seeking understanding. This monastery, your wisdom, the artifact – they were all guides on my path. But the journey doesn't end here."

The group gathered around a small fire, the flames flickering like the memories of their recent experiences. Aria, her empathic abilities now more refined, shared her insight. "This journey has shown us that our powers can create ripples beyond what we see. We must tread wisely."

Eldon, the seer, added, "The future is a web of possibilities. Our actions have shaped it for the better, but we must remain vigilant. The balance we've achieved is delicate."

The syndicate leader, now an ally, spoke with a tone of regret and hope. "I've been on the wrong side of this battle, blinded by my own ambition. But thanks to you all, especially Orion, I've seen a new path. One that seeks harmony rather than dominion."

Orion, looking at each member of the group, realized the depth of their shared bond. "We've all grown through this. Our paths may diverge, but the lessons we've learned and the bonds we've forged will remain."

As the night deepened, Orion reflected on his own path – the challenges faced, the truths uncovered, and the choices made. He understood that his journey was not just about confronting external threats but also about exploring the vast landscape within himself.

He turned to the group, his voice steady and clear. "Tomorrow, we part ways, each to our own calling. But let's not forget what brought us together and the strength we found in unity. Our paths may cross again, and when they do, may we be wiser and stronger."

The following morning, as the first light of dawn broke the darkness, Orion prepared to leave. The monastery, once a place of mystery, now felt like a part of his extended home. With a final look at the crystal cavern, a symbol of his journey, he stepped into the new day.

Orion's adventure in the Arctic was more than a physical quest; it was a spiritual and psychological odyssey that had deepened his character and enriched his understanding of his destiny and identity. The Crystal Cavern was no longer just a location on a map; it was a milestone in his life, a testament to the intricate dance of light and shadow, power and responsibility, action and introspection.

As he trekked through the snow, his cloak trailing behind him, Orion Nightshade carried with him not just the memories of the battles fought but also the wisdom gained, the friendships forged, and the realization that his journey was far from over.

The story of Orion's Legacy continued, with the Crystal Cavern standing as a beacon of his ever-evolving saga, a saga that beckoned to those who dared to venture into the unknown, seeking not just adventure but also the profound truths hidden within themselves and the world around them.

The Onyx Forge

Chapter 1

Orion Nightshade, cloaked in shadows, stood at the edge of the volcanic wasteland, his gaze fixed on the distant, smoldering peak where the Onyx Forge Monastery loomed like a sentinel over the fiery heart of the earth. The journey ahead was perilous, a path fraught with unknown dangers, but the allure of the monastery's ancient secrets pulled at him like a siren's call.

His journey had begun in a tavern nestled in the shadow of the volcano, where whispers of the monastery and its mystical blacksmith demigod had first reached his ears. A blend of fear and reverence colored the tales of the villagers, but to Orion, they were the missing pieces of a puzzle he'd long sought to solve. The amulet around his neck, a family heirloom, seemed to pulse with a life of its own, as if resonating with the energy of the volcano.

As Orion set out, the sun began its descent, painting the sky in hues of orange and crimson. The volcanic terrain was unforgiving, a labyrinth of jagged rocks and steep cliffs. Every step was a calculated risk, a dance with danger that Orion had mastered over the years. His agile form moved with cat-like grace, navigating the treacherous landscape with an ease that belied the effort involved.

The night fell swiftly, and with it came the creatures of the volcano. Shadowy figures, elemental beings born of fire and stone, emerged from the cracks and crevices, their glowing eyes fixed on the intruder. Orion's hand instinctively went to the hilt of his dagger, but he knew that steel would be of little use here. He whispered an ancient incantation, a gift from his amulet, and shadows coalesced around him, forming a barrier against the fiery assault.

The creatures hesitated, their fiery forms flickering uncertainly. Orion seized the moment, darting past them with supernatural speed, his cloak a blur of darkness against the fiery backdrop. The creatures roared in frustration, but

Orion was already beyond their reach, his heart pounding with exhilarating adrenaline.

As dawn broke, the volcano's peak loomed closer, its presence an oppressive weight in the air. Orion's journey took him through a village at the base of the mountain, where the locals regarded him with a mix of curiosity and fear. An old woman approached him, her eyes holding the wisdom of years.

"You seek the Onyx Forge," she stated, more than asked, her voice a raspy whisper.

Orion nodded, his eyes never leaving the peak. "I seek answers," he replied, his voice tinged with a resolve that had carried him through countless dangers.

"The path you walk is fraught with peril, young one," the woman warned, her gaze piercing. "The monastery is a place of secrets, and not all are meant to be uncovered."

Orion considered her words, feeling the weight of his quest. "Some secrets," he said slowly, "hold the key to understanding who we are, and what we are meant to be."

The woman nodded, a ghost of a smile touching her lips. "Then go forth, Orion Nightshade. May the shadows guide you and the fire reveal your truth."

Leaving the village behind, Orion continued his ascent. The air grew thinner, hotter, as he neared the peak. The monastery was now in sight, a formidable structure carved into the heart of the volcano. Its walls were blackened by centuries of volcanic activity, and the air around it shimmered with a heat that seemed almost alive.

As he approached the gates of the monastery, Orion felt a surge of energy from his amulet. It pulsed in time with his heartbeat, a steady rhythm that seemed to echo the heartbeat of the volcano itself. He reached out, pushing the heavy doors open, and stepped into the unknown.

The interior of the monastery was a stark contrast to the fiery outside world. The halls were cool and dimly lit, the air heavy with the scent of molten metal and ancient stone. The sound of hammers striking anvils echoed through the corridors, a symphony of creation that spoke of the monastery's purpose.

Orion moved silently through the halls, his senses alert to any sign of danger or discovery. He could feel the eyes of the monks on him, their gazes heavy with unspoken questions. But Orion had questions of his own, and he would not be deterred.

His journey had led him here, to the heart of the volcano, to the Onyx Forge Monastery. Here, he would find the answers he sought, or he would find his end. Either way, Orion Nightshade's destiny was irrevocably tied to the secrets that lay within these ancient walls.

Chapter 2

Orion Nightshade's footsteps echoed in the ancient halls of the Onyx Forge Monastery, the sound mingling with the distant clanging of metal and the soft murmurs of secretive conversations. The air was thick with the scent of smoldering embers and ancient stone, an aroma that spoke of untold mysteries and hidden knowledge. He felt the weight of many eyes upon him, the monks observing him with a cautious curiosity.

As he ventured deeper into the heart of the monastery, the temperature dropped, a stark contrast to the fiery exterior. The walls were adorned with intricate carvings depicting legendary battles and mythical creatures, each a testament to the monastery's storied past. Orion's fingers traced the lines of the carvings, feeling the pulsating energy that seemed to emanate from them.

Suddenly, he was accosted by a group of monks, their faces partially obscured by deep hoods. "You tread on sacred ground, outsider," one of them spoke, his voice a low rumble. "What purpose brings you to the Onyx Forge?"

Orion met their gaze squarely, his own eyes a reflection of the determination that had brought him this far. "I seek understanding," he replied, his voice steady. "Of this place, of the artifacts it guards, and of the amulet I bear."

The monks exchanged glances, a silent conversation passing between them. Finally, one stepped forward, his eyes revealing a glimmer of interest. "Your amulet," he said, gesturing towards the piece around Orion's neck. "It is not a common trinket. It carries the mark of ancient magic."

Orion touched the amulet, feeling its familiar contours. "It is a family heirloom," he explained, "linked to shadow magic. I believe its origins are connected to this place."

The monks whispered among themselves, their voices a hushed cadence. After a moment, the lead monk nodded. "Very well, Orion Nightshade. We will grant you access to our library. Perhaps there you will find the answers you seek."

The library of the Onyx Forge was a vast chamber, its walls lined with shelves that stretched into the shadows. Scrolls, tomes, and manuscripts of every conceivable age and origin filled the shelves, a treasure trove of knowledge.

Orion's eyes widened in awe as he perused the texts, each one a piece of history, a fragment of the world's magical lore. He dove into ancient scripts, deciphering languages long forgotten, each word bringing him closer to understanding the power of his amulet and the secrets of the Onyx Forge.

Hours turned to days as Orion immersed himself in the study. The monks observed him, their presence a constant reminder of the monastery's enigmatic nature. Occasionally, one would approach, offering insights into a particularly cryptic passage or a forgotten legend.

During one such interaction, a monk named Brother Lorian shared a tale that caught Orion's attention. "Long ago," Lorian began, "there was a blacksmith of unparalleled skill. He forged weapons of great power, but his greatest creation was said to be an amulet, one that harnessed the essence of shadow itself."

Orion listened intently, his heart racing. "This blacksmith," he asked, "could he be connected to the demigod rumored to reside here?"

Lorian nodded, a knowing look in his eyes. "The demigod you speak of is more than a mere rumor. He is the guardian of our forge, a being of immense power and wisdom. Perhaps he can shed light on your quest."

The revelation stirred a mixture of excitement and apprehension within Orion. The prospect of meeting a being of such power was daunting, yet it was a necessary step in unraveling the mystery of his amulet.

One evening, as the sun dipped below the horizon, bathing the monastery in a crimson glow, Orion was summoned to the heart of the forge. The heat was intense, the air vibrating with the energy of creation. There, amidst the flames and molten metal, stood the figure of the demigod blacksmith.

He was a towering presence, his physique radiating an aura of raw elemental power. His eyes, like molten gold, met Orion's with an intensity that seemed to peer into his very soul.

"Orion Nightshade," the demigod spoke, his voice resonating like the depths of the earth. "You seek answers about your amulet and its connection to the shadows. Why?"

Orion took a deep breath, steadying himself against the overwhelming presence of the demigod. "I seek to understand my heritage, the legacy of my family, and the role I am to play in the balance of this world's magic."

The demigod regarded him for a long moment, his gaze piercing. "Your quest is noble, but fraught with peril. The path of knowledge is not without its dangers, and the secrets you unearth may change you in ways you cannot yet comprehend."

Orion nodded, accepting the weight of the demigod's words. "I am prepared," he said, his voice firm. "Whatever it takes to uncover the truth."

The demigod's lips curled into a faint smile, an expression of both challenge and respect. "Very well, Orion Nightshade. Prepare yourself, for the journey ahead will test not only your physical strength but the very essence of your spirit."

As Orion left the forge, the amulet around his neck pulsed with a newfound energy, as if echoing the promise of revelations yet to come. The shadows around him seemed to dance with anticipation, and for the first time, Orion felt a deep connection to the ancient magic that coursed through his veins.

His journey at the Onyx Forge Monastery was just beginning, a path that would lead him not only towards understanding the mysteries of his amulet but also towards discovering his true destiny as a guardian of ancient powers.

Chapter 3

The heart of the Onyx Forge Monastery throbbed with the lifeblood of creation, a rhythm felt through the soles of Orion Nightshade's boots as he entered the forge. Towering anvils, flames leaping high, and the relentless clanging of hammer on metal dominated the space. The heat was oppressive, a palpable force that seemed to press against Orion's skin, but he moved forward, drawn by a force greater than the inferno around him.

There, amidst the chaos of creation, stood the blacksmith demigod, a figure of myth made flesh. His arms, like wrought iron, worked a glowing piece of metal with supernatural precision. Sparks flew with each strike, illuminating his features - a visage etched with the eternities of his craft.

Orion cleared his throat, his voice steady despite the awe he felt. "I seek the blacksmith demigod, guardian of the Onyx Forge."

The blacksmith paused, turning to face Orion. His eyes, reflecting the molten glow of the forge, bore into Orion. "I am he," he said, his voice a rumble like distant thunder. "What does the seeker of shadows want from me?"

Orion took a deep breath, feeling the heat of the forge as a physical weight. "I come to understand the legacy of my amulet and its connection to this place," he said, revealing the heirloom around his neck.

The demigod's gaze lingered on the amulet, a flicker of recognition in his eyes. "That amulet... it was forged here, long ago. It is entwined with your fate, Orion Nightshade, and with the destiny of this very forge."

Orion's heart raced. "Can you tell me about its creation? About the magic it holds?"

The blacksmith returned to his work, the rhythm of his hammering a hypnotic backdrop to his words. "That amulet was created for a purpose, to balance the light and dark. It was meant for a guardian, one who could wield the shadows without being consumed by them."

Orion felt a surge of questions, but the blacksmith raised a hand. "Patience. Understanding your amulet requires more than words. You must experience the essence of its creation."

With a gesture from the demigod, the flames of the forge flared, and an anvil illuminated by an ethereal light appeared. "Forge with me," the blacksmith commanded. "In the fire and metal, you will find your answers."

Orion stepped forward, the heat enveloping him like a second skin. He picked up the hammer offered to him, its handle fitting his grip as if made for him. Together, they worked the metal, Orion's every strike guided by the demigod's expert hand.

As metal took shape under his hammer, Orion felt a connection, a resonance with the amulet around his neck. It was as if each strike of the hammer peeled back layers of mystery, revealing glimpses of ancient wisdom and forgotten magic.

Hours passed, or perhaps it was moments - time seemed irrelevant in the forge's timeless embrace. Finally, as the last strike rang out, the piece was complete. It was not a weapon or a tool, but a symbol, a representation of balance - light and dark intertwined in harmony.

The blacksmith regarded the piece with an approving nod. "Your journey has just begun, Orion. The understanding you seek is not just about your amulet, but about yourself. You are a guardian, a keeper of balance. This forge, this monastery, they are part of your path, but only you can walk it."

Orion held the symbol, feeling a profound sense of purpose. "And the threat of the volcano?" he asked, recalling the tales of destruction.

The blacksmith's gaze turned towards the roaring flames. "The volcano is a force of nature, a symbol of the raw power we wield. It is not a threat, but a reminder - a reminder that power, like the elements, must be respected and balanced."

Orion nodded, his mind alight with newfound understanding and countless new questions. "Thank you," he said, bowing slightly to the demigod. "I will seek to understand, to balance the light and dark within me."

The blacksmith demigod smiled, a rare sight that seemed to soften his formidable presence. "Go forth, Orion Nightshade. The path of a guardian is solitary, but you are not alone. The legacy of the Onyx Forge is with you."

As Orion left the forge, the amulet pulsed with a warmth that matched the beating of his heart. He stepped into the cool night air, the stars above a tapestry of light amidst the darkness. The journey ahead was uncertain, filled with challenges and revelations, but Orion felt ready.

The secrets of the Onyx Forge had begun to unravel, and with them, the mysteries of his

own destiny. The path of a guardian, a protector of balance, lay ahead, and Orion Nightshade was ready to walk it.

Chapter 4

In the shadow of the Onyx Forge Monastery, Orion Nightshade faced a new dawn, one that promised not only enlightenment but also the gravest of trials. The blacksmith demigod had spoken of tests - challenges that would forge Orion's character as much as they would test his physical and magical abilities. Orion, standing at the threshold of this daunting journey, felt the weight of his destiny like never before.

As the morning sun broke over the volcanic landscape, bathing the monastery in a crimson hue, Brother Lorian approached Orion. "The trials you are about to face are ancient traditions of our order," he explained. "They are designed to test the limits of your body, mind, and spirit."

Orion nodded, his resolve firm. "I am ready," he said, his voice betraying none of the apprehension that churned within him.

The first trial was the Trial of Flames. Orion was led to a chamber deep within the monastery, where torrents of fire danced in a deadly ballet. His task was simple yet perilous: retrieve a sacred stone from the heart of the inferno.

Clad in his dark cloak, Orion stepped into the chamber. The heat was intense, a ravenous entity that sought to consume all in its path. Relying on his agility and the shadow magic that coursed through his veins, Orion danced through the flames, each movement a brush with death. The stone, glowing red-hot in the fire's heart, seemed an impossible prize. But with a burst of speed and a well-timed leap, Orion snatched it from the flames, emerging unscathed.

The monks, watching in silent awe, nodded in approval. But there was no time for rest. The second trial awaited.

The Trial of Shadows was a test of Orion's magical prowess. In a dimly lit chamber, shadows came to life, forming shapes and entities that mirrored Orion's deepest fears and doubts. Here, in this spectral arena, Orion had to confront and conquer his inner demons.

With each shadowy figure he faced, Orion dove deeper into his psyche, battling the manifestations of his past – the guilt of a thief, the uncertainty of a guardian, and the fear of a man walking a path fraught with unknown dangers. His amulet pulsed with each conquered fear, its power growing in tandem with his resolve.

As the last shadow dissipated, a sense of clarity enveloped Orion. He had faced his darkest fears and emerged stronger, his resolve hardened like steel in the forge.

But the final trial was yet to come - the Trial of Elements. Orion was led to the very heart of the volcano, where the elements of fire, earth, air, and water converged in a tumultuous symphony. His task was to harness these elements and forge a weapon symbolic of his journey.

Surrounded by the raw power of nature, Orion felt the energy of the elements coursing through him. He raised his hands, calling upon his newfound understanding of balance. Fire coalesced with air, earth mingled with water, and in a moment of transcendent clarity, Orion forged a blade that shimmered with elemental energy – a physical manifestation of his journey and growth.

As he emerged from the volcano, holding the blade aloft, the monks greeted him with a reverence reserved for those who had transcended the ordinary. Brother Lorian approached, a look of respect in his eyes. "You have passed the trials, Orion Nightshade. You are no longer just a seeker of knowledge. You are a guardian, a protector of the balance between light and dark."

Orion looked at the blade in his hands, its surface reflecting the myriad challenges he had overcome. He realized that these trials were not just tests of physical strength or magical ability; they were a journey of self-discovery, a crucible that had forged him into something more than he had been.

As the sun set, casting long shadows over the volcanic landscape, Orion stood at the edge of the monastery, gazing into the horizon. The path ahead was still shrouded in mystery, but he now walked it with a newfound purpose. The trials had revealed to him not just the depth of his powers, but also the strength of his spirit.

With the elemental blade in hand and the amulet pulsing steadily around his neck, Orion Nightshade was ready to face whatever the future held. The mysteries of the Onyx Forge awaited, and he was prepared to uncover them, to protect the balance that was now his to uphold.

Chapter 5

In the wake of his trials, Orion Nightshade found himself wrestling with a disquieting thought. The blacksmith demigod's immense power and mysterious aura had sown a seed of doubt in Orion's mind. Despite the demigod's role in guiding him through the trials, Orion couldn't shake off the suspicion that there might be a hidden agenda behind the façade of wisdom and guidance.

These thoughts consumed Orion as he wandered through the monastery's ancient corridors, the stone walls echoing with the whispers of ages past. His amulet, now more a part of him than ever, seemed to pulse in response to his turbulent thoughts.

Brother Lorian found him in the monastery's garden, a serene oasis amidst the volcanic turmoil. "You seem troubled, Orion," Lorian observed, his voice a gentle intrusion into Orion's brooding silence.

Orion looked up, the shadows in his eyes a stark contrast to the peaceful surroundings. "I can't help but wonder about the blacksmith demigod's true intentions. The power he wields... could it not be used for destruction as easily as for creation?"

Lorian considered his words carefully before responding. "Power is a tool, Orion. Like any tool, its nature depends on the hands that wield it. The demigod has been the guardian of the Onyx Forge for eons. His purpose has always been to maintain balance, not to destroy."

"But how can we be sure?" Orion pressed, his expression fraught with uncertainty. "What if there's more to his story, something hidden from us?"

"It is natural to fear what we do not understand," Lorian replied. "But remember, fear can cloud our judgment. Have faith in the path you have chosen and the guidance you have received."

Orion nodded, though the turmoil within him remained. He spent the following days observing the demigod from afar, scrutinizing his every move for any sign of deceit. He watched the demigod forge weapons of incredible power, each imbued with elemental magic. Yet, there was no malice in his work, only a deep concentration and a profound respect for his craft.

Despite this, Orion's suspicions led him down a dangerous path. One evening, under the cloak of darkness, he decided to confront the demigod directly. He found him in the forge, the flames casting dramatic shadows across his features.

"Why do you watch me with such suspicion, Orion Nightshade?" the demigod asked, his voice echoing in the vast chamber.

Orion stepped forward, his resolve steeling him. "I need to know if your intentions are truly noble. The power you possess could be used to awaken the volcano, to bring destruction upon the world."

The demigod set down his hammer and turned to face Orion fully. "Your fear blinds you," he said solemnly. "My purpose has always been to protect, to preserve the balance of elements. Awakening the volcano would bring imbalance and chaos, the very things I have sworn to prevent."

"Then why do you forge weapons of such power?" Orion challenged, his grip tightening on the hilt of his newly forged blade.

"To protect against greater threats," the demigod replied. "There are forces in this world, both seen and unseen, that seek to disrupt the balance we strive to maintain. These weapons are not instruments of destruction, but of protection."

Orion's stance softened slightly, his internal conflict evident. "And what of my role in all this? Why guide me through the trials?"

"Your journey is your own, Orion," the demigod said, his eyes reflecting the flames. "You have been chosen by forces greater than you or I. Your connection to the amulet, your mastery of shadow magic, all point to a destiny that intertwines with the fate of this world."

Orion absorbed his words, the weight of his destiny pressing upon him. The demigod's sincerity was apparent, his words resonating with a truth that Orion could not deny.

"Forgive my doubts," Orion finally said, his voice tinged with remorse. "I have been blinded by my own fears."

"There is no shame in doubt, Orion," the demigod reassured him. "It is a part of your journey, a test of your resolve. Embrace it, learn from it, and let it guide you towards the truth."

As Orion left the forge, the turmoil in his heart had eased. He realized that his suspicions, though misguided, were a necessary part of his path. They had not weakened him, but rather, they had strengthened his resolve to seek the truth and to fulfill his destiny.

The moon shone brightly over the Onyx Forge Monastery, casting a silver glow on its ancient walls. Orion Nightshade, once a thief in the shadows, now stood as a guardian of balance, his journey intertwined with the fate of a world where magic and reality were inseparably bound.

Chapter 6

After days of contemplation and internal conflict, Orion Nightshade's journey at the Onyx Forge Monastery took an unexpected turn. A new revelation was about to unfold, one that would challenge everything he thought he knew about the demigod blacksmith and the true purpose of the monastery.

It began with an invitation from the demigod himself, delivered by Brother Lorian. "The blacksmith demigod requests your presence at the heart of the forge tonight," Lorian conveyed, a hint of solemnity in his voice.

That evening, Orion descended into the depths of the monastery, the heat and the rhythmic pounding of the forge growing more intense with each step. He found the demigod waiting, his figure illuminated by the fiery glow of the forge.

"Orion Nightshade, you have proven yourself worthy through the trials," the demigod began, his voice resonating in the heated air. "But there is more you must understand. The true purpose of this forge, and my existence, extends beyond the forging of weapons."

Orion listened intently, his previous suspicions giving way to curiosity.

"This forge is not just a place of creation; it is a focal point of elemental balance," the demigod revealed. "The world is in a constant state of flux, a balance between the elemental forces. My role, and that of this forge, is to maintain this balance."

Orion's eyes widened in realization. The implications of this revelation were far-reaching. "The weapons... they are not just tools of war?"

"No," the demigod replied. "Each weapon I forge is imbued with elemental magic, designed to counteract imbalances in the world. When the elements are in discord, chaos ensues. These weapons help restore harmony."

The demigod led Orion to a balcony overlooking the volcano's fiery maw. "Look at this volcano. It is a symbol of nature's raw power, a reminder of the delicate balance we must uphold. If this balance is tipped, the consequences can be catastrophic."

Orion gazed into the volcano, the molten lava churning like a living thing. He realized the enormity of the demigod's task and the importance of the monastery's secret mission.

"But why me?" Orion asked, turning to the demigod. "Why involve me in this?"

"You are more than just a guardian of magical artifacts, Orion," the demigod said, his eyes reflecting the flames. "Your connection to the shadow magic, your ability to walk the line between light and dark, makes you integral to maintaining this balance. You are part of a larger destiny."

Orion took a deep breath, absorbing the weight of the demigod's words. His journey had brought him here for a reason. He was not just on a quest for personal understanding; he was a key player in a grander scheme.

"Your amulet," the demigod continued, pointing to the heirloom around Orion's neck, "is not a mere trinket. It is an ancient artifact of balance, capable of channeling and harmonizing elemental forces. You must learn to wield its power, not just for your sake, but for the world's."

Orion felt the amulet pulse against his chest, as if affirming the demigod's words. A sense of purpose, clearer than ever, filled him. He was no longer a mere adventurer or a seeker of knowledge. He was a protector, a guardian of the world's elemental balance.

"Teach me," Orion said, his voice steady and resolute.

The demigod nodded, a hint of a smile on his face. "Very well. Your training begins now."

In the weeks that followed, Orion trained under the demigod's guidance. He learned to harness the power of the elements, to channel them through his amulet, and to restore balance in small, controlled environments. Each lesson brought him closer to understanding his true role in the grand scheme of things.

One evening, as Orion stood on the balcony overlooking the volcano, he realized how much he had changed. The doubts and suspicions that had once clouded his mind were gone, replaced by a sense of clarity and purpose. He was no longer just Orion Nightshade, the thief-turned-guardian; he was a key figure in the eternal dance of the elements, a protector of the balance that held the world together.

As the moon rose over the Onyx Forge Monastery, casting its silver light on the volcanic landscape, Orion knew that his journey was far from over. There were still mysteries to unravel, challenges to face, and a destiny to fulfill. But he was ready, armed with knowledge, power, and a newfound understanding of his place in the world.

The legacy of the Onyx Forge was not just about forging weapons; it was about forging guardians - guardians like Orion Nightshade, who would stand as defenders of the world's elemental balance.

Chapter 7

The revelations about the Onyx Forge Monastery and its true purpose had set Orion Nightshade on a new path of discovery, particularly about his amulet, an ancient heirloom that had been his constant companion. The demigod's words about the amulet's power and significance had stirred a deep curiosity in Orion. It was time to unravel the mysteries of the amulet and understand its true legacy.

Orion sought out Brother Lorian, who had become a mentor and guide to him in the monastery. They met in the monastery's vast library, a place where the walls whispered ancient secrets.

"Brother Lorian, I need to understand more about my amulet," Orion began, the amulet glinting in the dim light of the library. "The demigod mentioned its connection to the elemental balance. Can you tell me more about its origins?"

Lorian led Orion to a secluded corner of the library, where ancient texts and scrolls lay in abundance. "Your amulet is more than just a family heirloom, Orion. It is an artifact of great power, forged centuries ago, at a time when the balance between light and dark was in peril."

Lorian carefully unrolled an ancient scroll, revealing detailed inscriptions and drawings. "See here," he pointed. "Your amulet is known as the 'Shadow Heart.' It was created by a coalition of mages and blacksmiths who sought to harness the power of shadow magic to maintain the world's balance."

Orion leaned closer, absorbing every detail. "Shadow Heart... so it is intrinsically linked to the balance of elements?"

"Yes," Lorian confirmed. "The Shadow Heart has the ability to channel and harmonize elemental forces. But its true power lies in its connection to the wearer. It amplifies the innate abilities of its bearer, particularly those attuned to shadow magic."

Orion pondered this, thinking back to the moments when he had felt the amulet resonate with his actions, guiding and amplifying his powers. "And my family? How did they come into possession of such an artifact?"

"The records are vague on this matter," Lorian admitted, rifling through another ancient tome. "But it is said that the Shadow Heart was passed down through generations, to those who showed a natural affinity for shadow magic and a strong sense of justice. Your family, the Nightshades, were chosen as its guardians, tasked with protecting its power and ensuring it was never misused."

Orion felt a surge of pride mixed with the weight of responsibility. His lineage was not just of thieves and shadow-walkers; they were guardians of a powerful legacy, protectors of the world's elemental balance.

Lorian closed the tome, his eyes meeting Orion's. "Orion, your journey to the Onyx Forge Monastery was no coincidence. It was destiny calling you to fulfill your role as the Shadow Heart's guardian. The trials you faced, the revelations you uncovered – all were steps leading you to this moment of understanding."

Orion stood, the pieces of his past falling into place like a puzzle. "What must I do now, Brother Lorian?"

"Embrace your heritage, Orion," Lorian advised. "Learn to wield the Shadow Heart's power to its fullest. The monastery will aid you in this endeavor. Your training has prepared you, but your journey is far from over."

Over the following weeks, Orion dedicated himself to understanding and mastering the Shadow Heart's power. He dove into ancient texts, practiced channeling elemental energies, and sought the demigod's guidance in harnessing the amulet's full potential.

One evening, as Orion stood at the edge of the volcano, he felt the amulet pulsate with a power that resonated with the very heartbeat of the earth. In that moment, he realized his true purpose. He was not just Orion Nightshade, the former thief and wandering adventurer. He was a guardian of balance, a wielder of ancient magic, and a protector of the elemental harmony that sustained the world.

As the moon cast its silver light over the monastery, Orion felt a newfound sense of belonging and purpose. The legacy of the Shadow Heart was now his to uphold, a legacy that bridged the gap between light and dark, magic and reality.

The journey ahead was uncertain, filled with challenges and dangers, but Orion Nightshade, with the Shadow Heart around his neck, was ready to face it all. For he was no longer alone; he was a part of something greater, a legacy that spanned generations and transcended time.

Chapter 8

As Orion Nightshade's understanding of his amulet deepened, so did his connection to the Onyx Forge Monastery. Yet, there were still secrets shrouded in the shadows of its ancient walls. Orion's quest for knowledge led him to dive deeper into the monastery's past and its mysterious connection to the elemental forces that governed the world.

One evening, while perusing the monastery's vast library, Orion stumbled upon a hidden passage behind a bookshelf. Curiosity piqued, he followed the narrow, dimly lit corridor that spiraled downwards into the heart of the monastery.

The passage opened into a cavernous chamber, illuminated by the soft glow of bioluminescent moss. In the center of the chamber stood a massive stone tablet, its surface etched with runes and symbols that Orion recognized as ancient elemental script.

As he approached the tablet, the amulet around his neck began to pulse with a warm light. The runes on the tablet started to glow in response, revealing a hidden narrative.

"The Onyx Forge was not just a monastery or a forge," Orion read aloud, his voice echoing in the chamber. "It was a seal, a containment for a rift in the elemental balance."

Orion's eyes widened in realization. The monastery was built atop a nexus point where elemental energies converged. The blacksmith demigod and the monks were not just weapon smiths; they were guardians of this nexus, maintaining the delicate balance between the elemental forces.

The tablet revealed more. Millennia ago, a cataclysmic event had threatened to disrupt the elemental balance, risking the world's descent into chaos. The Onyx Forge was established to prevent such a disaster from recurring. The weapons forged here were imbued with elemental magic, each serving as a key to stabilize the nexus point.

Orion traced his fingers over the runes, absorbing the history of the place he had come to respect. "So, the weapons... they are more than just tools of war. They are instruments of balance," he murmured to himself.

Lost in thought, Orion didn't hear Brother Lorian enter the chamber.

"Orion, you have discovered one of our most closely guarded secrets," Lorian said, his voice filled with a mix of surprise and respect.

Orion turned, the amulet glowing softly against his chest. "I had my suspicions, but I never imagined the full extent of the monastery's purpose."

Lorian walked over to the stone tablet, his gaze reflective. "This knowledge was to be revealed to you in time. Your connection to the amulet, your role as a guardian, it's all intertwined with the destiny of the Onyx Forge."

Orion looked at Lorian, a newfound sense of responsibility settling upon him. "What role am I to play in all this? How does the amulet fit into the monastery's purpose?"

Lorian placed a hand on Orion's shoulder. "You, Orion Nightshade, are a key to maintaining the elemental balance. Your amulet, the Shadow Heart, has the unique ability to harmonize the elemental energies. You are destined to be more than a guardian of artifacts; you are to be a protector of the balance itself."

Overwhelmed by the revelation, Orion felt the weight of his destiny heavier than ever. "And the demigod blacksmith?"

"He is your mentor and guide in this journey," Lorian explained. "Together, you must work to ensure the stability of the elemental forces. There will be trials, challenges that will test your strength and resolve. But I believe you are ready for them."

Orion nodded, a sense of purpose igniting within him. "I will do whatever it takes to protect the balance."

As he left the chamber, the secrets of the Onyx Forge firmly etched in his mind, Orion felt a shift within him. He was no longer just a seeker of truth; he was a defender of a legacy that spanned millennia. The path ahead was fraught with uncertainty, but Orion Nightshade was ready to face it, armed with the knowledge and power of the Onyx Forge and the Shadow Heart.

The moon cast its silver light through the monastery's windows, bathing the ancient stone in a mystical glow. Orion stood there, gazing into the night, his heart and mind aligned with the monumental task that lay ahead. The secrets unveiled had changed him, forging him into a guardian of a legacy that was not just his own, but that of the world itself.

Chapter 9

In the tranquil gardens of the Onyx Forge Monastery, Orion Nightshade found himself alone with his thoughts. The revelations about the monastery, the elemental balance, and the true purpose of his amulet had reshaped his understanding of his journey. The moon cast a soft glow over the volcanic landscape, and the gentle rustling of leaves in the night wind accompanied Orion's contemplative mood.

He sat on a stone bench, gazing at the amulet in his hand. The Shadow Heart, as Brother Lorian called it, was not just a link to his past but a key to a much larger destiny. Orion pondered the weight of this responsibility, the role he was destined to play in maintaining the balance of the world.

His journey had been a tapestry of challenges and revelations. From a skilled thief in the shadows to a guardian of ancient powers, Orion's transformation was profound. Yet, beneath the surface of this newfound purpose, lay the remnants of his former life – doubts, fears, and unanswered questions about his identity.

Orion recalled his childhood, the early years of training in the art of stealth and thievery under his father's guidance. Back then, life was a game of shadows, a dance on the edge of danger. But now, his path had led him to a crossroads, where the shadows merged with the light of greater understanding.

"The path of a guardian is solitary, but you are not alone," the demigod blacksmith's words echoed in his mind. Orion realized that his journey was not just about self-discovery but about embracing his role in a larger narrative. He was a part of something ancient, something vital to the world's harmony.

As he reflected on his experiences at the monastery, Orion understood that his trials were not merely tests of skill or strength but lessons in understanding the delicate balance of the world. His initial suspicions of the demigod, the trials of fire, shadows, and elements – all were steps towards understanding the intricate dance of light and dark, order and chaos.

Orion's gaze shifted to the volcano, its presence a constant reminder of the raw power of nature and the fine line between creation and destruction. He thought about the elemental forces, the weapons forged by the demigod, and the role he was to play in maintaining the balance.

The monastery had become more than a place of learning; it was a sanctuary where Orion had found purpose and direction. The monks, once mysterious figures, were now his mentors and allies in a shared mission. And the demigod, initially a figure shrouded in suspicion, had become a guide and a source of wisdom.

Orion realized that his identity was not defined by his past as a thief or the shadows he once embraced. It was shaped by the choices he made, the challenges he faced, and the destiny he accepted. He was Orion Nightshade, the guardian of the Shadow Heart, a protector of the balance between magic and reality.

As the night deepened, Orion felt a sense of peace settle over him. The journey ahead would be fraught with challenges, but he was no longer the lone wanderer he once was. He was a part of a legacy that transcended time, a guardian of a balance that was the heartbeat of the world.

The moon's silver light shone on the Shadow Heart, reflecting a spectrum of colors in its intricate design. Orion stood, a renewed sense of resolve in his steps. He was ready to embrace his destiny, to protect the world's elemental balance, and to continue his journey of discovery, magic, and self-realization.

The Onyx Forge Monastery, with its ancient secrets and mystical powers, had become a home to Orion Nightshade. And as he walked back towards the monastery, the shadows and light danced around him, a symbol of the eternal balance he was sworn to protect.

Chapter 10

The morning sun cast a golden hue over the Onyx Forge Monastery, signaling the dawn of a significant day for Orion Nightshade. Today, he would face the Forge's Test, a critical challenge that would merge his shadow magic with the elemental powers of the volcano. The test was not only a rite of passage but a crucial step in his journey as a guardian.

Orion stood in the central courtyard, where the demigod blacksmith and the monks had gathered. The air was thick with anticipation. The demigod approached Orion, his eyes reflecting the seriousness of the moment.

"Orion Nightshade, the time has come for you to face the Forge's Test," the demigod announced. "You must harness the elemental energies of the volcano, channeling them through your amulet. This will not be an easy task. Are you prepared?"

Orion nodded, feeling the weight of the amulet around his neck. "I am ready."

The demigod led Orion to the edge of the volcano. The ground rumbled softly beneath their feet, a reminder of the raw power that lay dormant within. Orion could feel the heat emanating from the earth, the air tinged with sulfur.

"Focus on your connection with the Shadow Heart," the demigod instructed. "Let it guide you to channel the elemental energies."

Orion closed his eyes, taking a deep breath. He reached within himself, tapping into the shadow magic that he had honed over the years. The amulet began to glow, a soft light emanating from its core.

As Orion opened himself to the elemental energies, he felt a surge of power flow through him. The volcano's heart beat in rhythm with his own, its fiery essence merging with the shadows within him. He raised his hands, and the ground trembled, responding to his command.

"Control the energy, Orion. Do not let it overwhelm you," the demigod cautioned.

Orion struggled to maintain balance. The power was immense, threatening to consume him. He remembered the teachings of the monks, the lessons of balance and harmony. Gradually, he began to channel the energy, directing it through the amulet.

The air crackled with electricity, and a column of fire erupted from the volcano, reaching towards the sky. Orion, at the center of this maelstrom of energy, remained calm, his focus unwavering.

The demigod watched in awe, realizing the extent of Orion's abilities. The monks whispered among themselves, witnessing a guardian come into his true power.

Finally, Orion lowered his hands, and the column of fire dissipated. The ground stilled, and the air cooled. He opened his eyes, the amulet still glowing, now with a steady light.

"You have passed the Forge's Test, Orion Nightshade," the demigod declared, his voice filled with respect. "You have proven your ability to wield the elemental powers in harmony with your shadow magic. You are truly a guardian of the balance."

The monks approached, offering their congratulations. Orion felt a sense of accomplishment, but also a deeper understanding of his role. The test had shown him the potential of his powers and the responsibility that came with it.

"Your journey is far from over, Orion," the demigod said, placing a hand on his shoulder. "There will be challenges ahead, moments of doubt and danger. But remember this day, the day you embraced your destiny as a guardian of the elemental balance."

Orion nodded, his gaze fixed on the volcano. He had faced the Forge's Test and emerged stronger, more attuned to his purpose. The path ahead was uncertain, but he was ready to face whatever came his way.

As the day came to an end, Orion stood alone, looking out over the volcanic landscape. The test had changed him, not just in power, but in spirit. He was no longer a wanderer in the shadows; he was a beacon of balance, a protector of the world's elemental harmony.

The sun set behind the mountains, casting a warm glow over the monastery. Orion Nightshade, with the Shadow Heart around his neck, was ready for the next chapter of his journey, a journey that would take him beyond the Onyx Forge, into the heart of the world's mysteries.

Chapter 11

The heart of the Onyx Forge Monastery throbbed with a palpable energy, as if the very core of the volcano was aligning with Orion Nightshade's newfound strength. The successful completion of the Forge's Test had marked a pivotal transformation in Orion. He was no longer just a guardian of artifacts; he had become an embodiment of the elemental balance he was destined to protect.

As he stood in the inner sanctum of the monastery, the eyes of the demigod blacksmith and the monks upon him, Orion felt a profound connection to the world's elemental forces. The air around him crackled with the energy he had harnessed, his shadow magic now perfectly intertwined with the fiery essence of the volcano.

The demigod blacksmith, his expression a mix of admiration and awe, approached Orion. "You have embraced the flame, Orion Nightshade. You have achieved what many thought impossible. The balance of elemental forces now resides within you."

Orion nodded, feeling the warm glow of the amulet against his skin. "I understand now. My journey, my purpose, it's greater than I ever imagined."

The demigod smiled. "Indeed. But with great power comes great responsibility. You must use this power to maintain the balance, to protect the world from those who would seek to disrupt it."

The monks gathered around, their expressions solemn yet hopeful. One of them, an elder with wise eyes, stepped forward. "Orion, your transformation has not only changed you but also the destiny of our monastery. We are custodians of ancient secrets, and with your newfound abilities, you can help us preserve these for future generations."

Orion felt the weight of his duty, a responsibility that extended beyond himself. "I will do everything in my power to uphold the balance and protect the secrets of the Onyx Forge."

As the day turned to evening, a ceremony was held in Orion's honor. The monks chanted ancient hymns, their voices echoing through the monastery, blending with the rumbling of the volcano. The energy of the place seemed to resonate with the newfound power within Orion.

During the ceremony, the demigod blacksmith presented Orion with a weapon forged in the heart of the volcano. "This is not just a weapon," the demigod explained. "It is a symbol of your guardianship, a tool that will aid you in maintaining the elemental balance."

Orion took the weapon, feeling its heat and power. It was a sword, its blade shimmering with a fiery glow, reflecting the flames of the forge. He knew that this sword was more than a mere object; it was a part of him now, a manifestation of his bond with the elemental forces.

That night, as Orion sat alone, gazing into the heart of the volcano, he contemplated his journey. He had come to the monastery seeking answers, only to find a purpose far greater than he had imagined. The challenges he had faced had not only tested his physical and magical abilities but had also forced him to confront his inner demons, his doubts, and fears.

Now, as a guardian of the elemental balance, he knew his journey was far from over. There would be trials ahead, adversaries who sought to tip the scales in their favor, and moments of doubt. But Orion felt ready. He had embraced the flame, and in doing so, had found his true calling.

As the moon rose over the volcanic landscape, casting a silver glow over the monastery, Orion felt a sense of peace. He had found his place in the world, not as a thief or a wanderer in the shadows, but as a protector of the balance, a guardian of the ancient powers that governed the world.

Tomorrow, he would begin a new chapter in his journey, but for tonight, he allowed himself to bask in the warmth of the fire, the steady heartbeat of the volcano, and the knowledge that he was exactly where he was meant to be. In the heart of the Onyx Forge, Orion Nightshade had found his home.

Chapter 12

The dawn at the Onyx Forge Monastery was unlike any other, its rays illuminating the volcanic landscape with a golden hue. Orion Nightshade stood at the edge of a precipice overlooking the vast expanse, his heart filled with a mixture of fulfillment and anticipation. The journey that had brought him here, to this moment of profound understanding and power, was etched deeply into his soul.

As he watched the sunrise, the Blacksmith Demigod joined him, his presence as formidable and enigmatic as ever. "Orion, you have come far," he said, his voice resonating with the wisdom of ages. "Your journey has only just begun."

Orion turned to face him, his eyes reflecting the light of the dawn. "I understand that now. The balance I hold within me is not just for the Onyx Forge, but for the world beyond."

The demigod nodded. "Indeed. The world is in a constant state of flux, and you, Orion Nightshade, are now its guardian. But remember, with great power comes the need for vigilance and humility."

Orion felt the weight of his new role, a responsibility that extended beyond the walls of the monastery. "I will protect the balance with everything I have. But where do I go from here? How do I begin?"

The demigod's gaze turned towards the horizon. "Your path is your own to choose. The world is vast, and its mysteries many. Trust your instincts, they have brought you this far."

As the morning progressed, the monks of the monastery gathered to bid Orion farewell. Each monk offered words of wisdom and tokens of their esteem.

The elder monk, who had been a mentor to Orion throughout his trials, approached with a small, intricately carved box.

"Orion, within this box lies a map of ancient ley lines, the lifeblood of our world's magic. It will guide you to places where the balance may need your attention," the elder explained, his eyes filled with pride and hope.

Orion accepted the box with reverence. "Thank you. I will honor the trust you have placed in me."

The villagers from the surrounding region also came to see him off, their faces showing a mixture of awe and gratitude. They had come to see Orion not just as a guardian of the monastery but as a protector of their homes and lives.

One young girl, her eyes wide with wonder, stepped forward. "Will you come back, Orion?" she asked timidly.

Orion knelt before her, his smile gentle. "I may travel far, but the Onyx Forge and its people will always be a part of me. I will return, in times of need."

As Orion prepared to depart, he felt a surge of energy from the amulet around his neck. It pulsed with a steady rhythm, like a heartbeat, reminding him of the interconnectedness of all things. The elemental balance he carried within him was not a burden, but a gift, a purpose that transcended his former life as a thief.

Standing at the threshold of the monastery, Orion took one last look at the place that had transformed him. He then stepped out, his cloak billowing in the mountain wind, the ancient amulet glowing softly against his chest.

The world lay before him, vast and uncharted, filled with mysteries and wonders yet to be discovered. Orion Nightshade, once a lone thief in the shadows, was now a guardian of elemental balance, a protector of the ancient and mystical. His journey had changed him in ways he could never have imagined, and now, a new chapter awaited.

With a determined stride, Orion began his descent down the mountain, each step taking him further into his destiny. The legacy of the Onyx Forge was now a part of him, and he, in turn, was a part of its enduring legacy.

As he vanished into the mists of the morning, the monks watched, knowing that the world was a little safer, a little more balanced, with Orion Nightshade as its guardian. The legacy of the Onyx Forge continued, not just in the heart of the volcano, but in the heart of a man who had embraced his destiny to protect the balance between magic and reality.

Check out more of Orion's adventures in Part II